SHATTERING EXPERIENCE

Kay Lewis walked around the room of the self-defense center to one of the mats lying near the front window. "This is a good spot here. We'll need plenty of room for this."

"For what?" Joe asked warily.

"It's a surprise," Kay said with a smile. "If I told you, I'd lose the advantage of sur—"

Her words were cut off by a loud crash. The window next to her exploded, and shards of glass flew across the room.

Something shattered on the floor next to the mat Kay was standing on.

Frank heard a muffled *whump*—and a wall of fire erupted around Kay Lewis!

Books in THE HARDY BOYS CASEFILES™ Series

#1 DEAD ON TARGET
#2 EVIL, INC.
#3 CULT OF CRIME
#4 THE LAZARUS PLOT
#5 EDGE OF DESTRUCTION
#6 THE CROWNING TERROR
#7 DEATHGAME
#8 SEE NO EVIL
#9 THE GENIUS THIEVES
#10 HOSTAGES OF HATE
#11 BROTHER AGAINST BROTHER
#12 PERFECT GETAWAY
#13 THE BORGIA DAGGER
#14 TOO MANY TRAITORS
#15 BLOOD RELATIONS
#16 LINE OF FIRE
#17 THE NUMBER FILE
#18 A KILLING IN THE MARKET
#19 NIGHTMARE IN ANGEL CITY
#20 WITNESS TO MURDER
#21 STREET SPIES
#22 DOUBLE EXPOSURE
#23 DISASTER FOR HIRE
#24 SCENE OF THE CRIME
#25 THE BORDERLINE CASE
#26 TROUBLE IN THE PIPELINE
#27 NOWHERE TO RUN
#28 COUNTDOWN TO TERROR
#29 THICK AS THIEVES
#30 THE DEADLIEST DARE
#31 WITHOUT A TRACE
#32 BLOOD MONEY
#33 COLLISION COURSE
#34 FINAL CUT
#35 THE DEAD SEASON
#36 RUNNING ON EMPTY
#37 DANGER ZONE
#38 DIPLOMATIC DECEIT
#39 FLESH AND BLOOD
#40 FRIGHT WAVE
#41 HIGHWAY ROBBERY
#42 THE LAST LAUGH
#43 STRATEGIC MOVES
#44 CASTLE FEAR
#45 IN SELF-DEFENSE

Available from ARCHWAY Paperbacks

THE HARDY BOYS CASEFILES NO. 45

IN SELF-DEFENSE

FRANKLIN W. DIXON

AN ARCHWAY PAPERBACK
Published by POCKET BOOKS
New York London Toronto Sydney Tokyo Singapore

An ARCHWAY PAPERBACK *Original*

An Archway Paperback published by
POCKET BOOKS, a division of Simon & Schuster Inc.
1230 Avenue of the Americas, New York, NY 10020

Produced by Mega-Books of New York, Inc.

ISBN: 0-671-70042-1

First Archway Paperback printing November 1990

10 9 8 7 6 5 4 3 2 1

Printed in the U.S.A.

IL 7+

Chapter 1

"SHE'S DOING *WHAT?*" Joe Hardy asked in disbelief. He rolled up the van window and ran his hand through his windblown blond hair. He shifted his clear blue eyes from the passing buildings to his brother in the driver's seat.

Frank Hardy didn't answer right away. They were stuck in the early evening traffic rush, and he was going over a mental checklist of routes that might bypass the tangle of cars on the main streets of Bayport.

Frank knew more about the back roads and shortcuts in his hometown than any street map would ever reveal. He made his decision, flicked the turn signal, and made a smooth left turn just as the stoplight shifted from yellow to red.

"Callie's taking a self-defense course," Frank finally said as he pushed the van up to the speed limit. His window was open a crack, and air whistled in, ruffling his brown hair. He didn't look at his brother to see his reaction, but there was a twinkle in his brown eyes as he pretended to concentrate on the road. "What's wrong with that?"

Joe snorted softly to himself. Frank had been going with Callie Shaw for a long time, and Joe had nothing against her. In fact, he sort of admired her in some ways. Of course, he would never admit that to anyone.

"A self-defense class for girls," he muttered. "They'll probably sit around talking for an hour, and then the instructor will hand out cute little tear-gas canisters on key chains."

"It's not just for girls," Frank replied. "And the instructor's got some pretty serious martial arts experience—including a third-degree black belt in karate."

Joe raised his eyebrows. "Why don't *you* teach her?" Joe suggested. "You know karate."

"I'm no expert," Frank said. "I've still got a lot to learn."

Joe shot a sidelong glance at his older brother. "You're not thinking of signing up for this class, are you?"

Frank shrugged. "I don't know. It might be interesting. The first class is tonight, and I thought I might check it out. Want to come along?"

Joe shook his head. "No, thanks. I can think of better ways to waste my time."

"You might learn something," Frank said.

"That's what *school* is for," Joe replied. "I've got nothing against it—but I like to take a break once in a while."

"Too bad," Frank said. "We're going out for pizza later." He paused for a second and then added, "I'm buying."

Joe glanced out the window. The sun had already set, and the dim half-light of dusk was quickly fading to darkness. "All right. What time does it start?"

"I'm supposed to meet Callie there at six-thirty," Frank answered.

Joe checked the clock on the dashboard. It read 6:15. "Kind of short notice," he observed. "What would you do if I said no and you had to drop me off at home first?"

Frank eased the black van to a stop at a red light. He turned to his brother and grinned. "Either I'd be late—or you'd have a long walk."

As soon as Frank parked the van in front of the address Callie had given him Joe hopped out and looked around. A sign on the large plate-glass front window of the two-story brick building identified it as the home of the AAA Self-defense Center.

Joe noticed that the building stood out because it was one of the few on the block that had any lights on. He looked up and down the block. Half the streetlights were either burnt out or broken, making the shadows cast by the few working lights seem harsh and ugly.

Across the street was a building with boarded-up windows. On the roof there was an old billboard that said "Your Ad Here." The strips peeling off the sign told Joe that no one had pasted the name of an exciting, new, improved product up there in a long time.

That hardly surprised him. Except for the bank on the corner most of the buildings on the block seemed abandoned, the dark windows and doorways adding to the gloom.

"Good spot for a self-defense school," he said as Frank joined him on the sidewalk. "Around here you'd probably get mugged going out for the mail."

Frank spied a large form passing under a street lamp and crossing over to their side of the street. Frank nodded in the direction of the approaching figure. "Looks like somebody is still willing to risk it." He nudged his brother. "Maybe it's one of those muggers."

Joe whirled, ready to attack, and the figure froze. "Joe? Frank?" a familiar voice called out. "What are you doing here?"

"That's no mugger," Joe said. "That's Chet Morton."

Chet walked up to the Hardys. If anybody could take care of himself on a dark, deserted street, it was Chet Morton. Some people mistook Chet's bulk for fat. Frank knew better. Chet wasn't going to win any Mr. Universe contests, but his massive form did pack a lot of muscle.

"You're not exactly close to home, either," Frank said. "What brings you to this scenic neighborhood?"

"Yeah," Joe added. "You don't see too many upwardly mobile young bankers prowling around this part of town."

"That's right," Frank said. "I forgot. You've got a part-time job as a bank teller."

Chet nodded and pointed over his shoulder with his thumb. "That's the bank down there on the corner. I just got off work. I saw this school's sign a couple of weeks ago, and I figured it wouldn't hurt to learn a few karate moves. Breaking boards with my bare hands would be a great trick at parties, don't you think?"

"I can't believe there's a bank around here," Joe commented.

"This used to be a nice area," Chet said. "And the Bayport Savings Bank has been here for over thirty years."

Frank glanced at his watch. "We'd better head inside."

"What's the rush?" Joe asked. "Let's stay out here a little longer and soak up the ambience of this wonderful neighborhood."

"You can stay out there and soak until you're all wet," a female voice called from the front door of the building. The voice was Callie Shaw's. "But your brother might be more interested in what goes on inside. Come on, Frank. The class is about to start."

As they went in Joe turned to Callie and said, "I'm only here because Frank bribed me."

Callie flashed her sparkling eyes at him. "What's

the matter?" she replied coolly, with a toss of her blond hair. "Afraid you might learn something?"

They walked into a large open room. Frank did a quick scan of the layout. One wall was mostly covered by the wide, plate-glass front window. The other walls were bare. There were heavy padded mats on the floor and some folding chairs. That was about it. Frank steered his brother toward a couple of seats in the back while Callie and Chet joined a small group of people near the front.

A woman walked in wearing a traditional karate outfit—a white robe with a sash around the waist and baggy white pants. Since she was the only person dressed that way, Frank knew she must be the instructor.

She didn't exactly fit Frank's vision of a martial arts expert. She was short and stocky. She didn't look much older than twenty—but Frank guessed that her round face and short, dark blond hair made her look younger than she probably was. There was a smooth, catlike confidence in her stride, and Frank had a feeling this was not a lady to mess with.

The woman walked quietly to the front of the room and faced the class. "My name is Kay Lewis," she announced.

Joe leaned over to his brother. "I should have known," he whispered. "It's just like Callie to try to learn martial arts from someone who looks like she just got out of high school."

"Shhh!" Frank hissed. "I want to hear what she says."

"Welcome to the Triple-A Self-defense Center," Kay Lewis continued, her eyes sweeping the small crowd. "I assume most of you are here because you want to learn something about self-defense." Her alert gaze rested briefly on the Hardys. "And some of you just want to find out what this place is all about.

"This is a free introductory session. If you like what you see and hear, the real training starts the day after tomorrow—and then we meet three times a week for the next four weeks.

"But before you spend any money you should know what you're getting into. And the first thing you should know is what self-defense is *not*. It is not an art, a ritual, or a life-style. You don't have to practice every day for the rest of your life, and you don't have to call me master or *sensei*."

Chet Morton raised his hand.

She turned to him and said, "I'll take questions in a minute. But if I stop now, I'll forget the little speech I memorized." Frank was impressed with her poise and control. "Don't worry," she added, "it won't take long. I haven't learned lung-fu yet."

She paused again. "That's the ancient art of talking your opponent to death."

Everybody in the room cracked up—including Joe.

After they settled down, she resumed. "Self-defense is also not a sport or a contest. There are no rules, and nobody keeps score. There are no winners—only survivors.

"There is no special equipment, and there are no exotic weapons. Most of you probably already own the best self-defense gear ever made—a good pair of running shoes."

"Are you saying you should run away from a fight?" Joe blurted out.

"Absolutely," she replied firmly. "The main goal of self-defense is to survive an attack. The best way to do that is to put a healthy distance between you and the attacker."

"What if you're not wearing running shoes?" Joe shot back. "Or there's no place to run?"

Kay Lewis smiled. "That's what this course is all about. And that's the end of my little speech." She shifted her attention to Chet Morton. "I think you had a question."

"I think you already answered it," Chet said glumly. "I guess we won't be learning how to break boards with our bare hands."

She shrugged her shoulders. "That depends."

"On what?" Chet asked hopefully.

"On whether or not vicious gangs of lumber are a serious problem around here."

The whole room broke out in laughter again. Then there was a loud *crack!* like a gunshot. All the laughter stopped abruptly.

Frank was the only one who wasn't startled

by the noise. He had been watching Kay Lewis when she swiftly clapped her hands over her head. With one simple motion she had the undivided attention of everyone in the room.

"That's your first lesson," she said. "Surprise is your secret weapon. Never signal your intentions to your opponent."

She looked at the faces around her. "I need a couple of volunteers for a little demonstration." Several hands went up, but she ignored them. "How about you two in the back?" she called out.

"Who? Us?" Joe responded in surprise. He shook his head. "I don't think so."

"What's the matter? Afraid I can take you?" It wasn't a question. It was a challenge.

Joe started to rise—but Frank put out his hand and stopped him. "Why us?"

"Because you fit the profile," Kay Lewis replied. "A couple of young guys who look like they're in pretty good shape. There aren't too many female muggers prowling the streets.

"And in case you hadn't noticed," she added, "this class hasn't exactly attracted a lot of guys."

Frank *had* noticed. In fact, other than Chet Morton they were the only males in the room. "I think you should know," he said, "that I've studied karate."

"Let's see what you've got," Kay Lewis said simply. She seemed unfazed by Frank's statement.

Frank shrugged. "Okay," he said as he stood up. "What do you want us to do?"

Kay walked around the room to one of the mats lying near the front window. "This is a good spot here. We'll need plenty of room for this."

"For what?" Joe asked warily.

"It's a surprise," Kay said with a smile. "If I told you, I'd lose the advantage of sur—"

Her words were cut off by a loud crash. The window next to her exploded, and shards of glass flew across the room.

Something shattered on the floor next to the mat Kay Lewis was standing on. Frank heard a muffled *whump*—and a wall of fire erupted around Kay Lewis.

Chapter 2

FRANK LEAPT UP and started toward the fire, but Kay Lewis was already diving through the flames. She hit the floor in a roll. She was fast—but not fast enough. Frank could see that her clothing was already on fire.

Frank grabbed one of the heavy mats off the floor and dragged it toward her. He draped the mat over her and threw himself on top of it, smothering the flames.

Joe and Callie were moving, too. They picked up another one of the bulky mats and threw it on the fire. The air filled with acrid smoke and the reek of burning plastic, but the fire was out almost as fast as it had begun.

"I think you can get this thing off me now," a muffled voice said.

Frank realized that he was still holding the mat around Kay in a bear hug.

"It's all right," she assured him with a straight face. "I promise not to burst into flames again. Really."

"Are you okay?" Frank asked as he pulled the mat off her.

She got up slowly, held out her arms, and looked down at her white robe and pants, now singed with black smudges. "I think so—thanks to you."

"That was some demonstration," Joe said. "What kind of show do you do on the Fourth of July?"

"What happened?" Chet called out.

Frank had almost forgotten there were other people in the room. He turned and saw Chet and a few others still sitting in their chairs. It had all happened so fast, they were too stunned even to move.

Joe looked down at the floor. Stooping, he carefully brushed away some shards of glass and uncovered the jagged remains of a broken bottle. He caught a whiff of gasoline. "I thought this was a beginners' class," he said.

Kay gave him a puzzled look.

Joe held out the bottle. "Defending yourself against Molotov cocktails is strictly an *advanced* technique."

The puzzled look remained on her face.

"A crude firebomb," Frank explained. "Just fill a bottle with gasoline, stuff a rag in the top, light it, throw it, and boom!"

"I know what a Molotov cocktail is," Kay responded. "But I wouldn't expect a couple of high school students to know how to make one."

"You never know when it might come in handy," Joe said blandly.

Frank smiled. "You'd be surprised by the things we know. Solving crimes is a kind of hobby of ours."

Kay's eyes narrowed. "A hobby? Just who are you guys, anyway?"

"They came with me," Callie interjected. "Kay Lewis, meet Frank and Joe Hardy. They can't help being nosy—it's in the blood. Their father's a detective."

"Made any enemies lately?" Frank asked, studying Kay's face.

"Women in the martial arts don't make a lot of friends," she answered vaguely.

"We'd better call the police," Joe said.

Kay nodded. "The phone's in the other room."

"I'll take care of it," Callie said, putting her hand on Kay's arm. "You sit down and take it easy."

A few minutes later Con Riley and another officer showed up. Frank and Joe weren't surprised. Con was one of the hardest-working cops on the Bayport police force. When there was trouble, Con Riley was usually one of the first officers on the scene.

Con scanned the damage quickly and then shifted his attention to Kay Lewis. "I was afraid something like this might happen," he said grimly.

"Do you know something we don't?" Joe asked.

"Probably," Riley replied. "But it's police business, Joe. I know you guys are just trying to help, but Chief Collig would be a lot happier if you two would find some other way to occupy your time."

"It's all right," Kay said. "I wouldn't be talking to you now if these guys hadn't been around."

She turned to the Hardys. "A few months ago, just after I bought this building and opened the school, I received a couple of weird letters."

"Weird?" Frank cut in. "What do you mean?"

"Threats," Con Riley said.

"What kind of threats?" Frank prodded.

"Oh, you know," Kay replied, trying to sound casual. "Just your basic get-out-of-town-or-else threats. I turned them over to the police, and that was the end of it."

"Until now," Joe added.

"Got any leads?" Frank asked.

Con Riley shrugged. "Not really. There's a local gang—the Scorpions. They made a lot of noise about a martial arts school being on their turf. But we don't have anything solid."

"I run into them on the streets sometimes," Kay said. "They practice their tough-guy glares on me, but that's about it.

"They hang out at the video arcade over on Becking Street," she continued. "Right after I started getting the letters I went over there and had a talk with their leader—a guy named Conrad Daye."

"Conrad Daye?" Frank responded. He recognized the name.

Riley snorted. "He's got a rap sheet a yard long."

"You actually just walked in there and confronted him?" Joe asked Kay.

"I didn't say I confronted him," she answered. "I said I had a *talk* with him."

"So what did you find out?" Frank said, trying to steer the conversation back on course.

"He didn't admit anything," Kay said. "But he didn't deny anything, either."

Con Riley took their statements, and his partner picked up the remains of the gasoline bomb. By the time the police had finally left, most of the people who had come for the class were long gone.

"I don't think too many of them will come back again," Kay said with a weak smile.

"I'll be back," Callie replied firmly. "And I think most of the others will be, too."

"Yeah," Chet agreed as they walked to the door. "That was pretty cool, the way you jumped through those flames."

They all walked outside. "Do you live here?" Frank asked Kay.

"Not yet," she answered. "But in a couple of weeks I'll have the apartment on the second floor all fixed up. Then I won't have to drive to work anymore."

Frank was about to ask another question when a car pulled up to the curb.

"Oh, no," Kay groaned softly. "Not again."

Frank tensed. "Trouble?" he whispered.

Kay chuckled. "Yeah—but not the kind you think. Don't worry, I can handle it."

Joe watched a man in a neatly pressed suit get out of the car. His dark hair was streaked with gray at the temples. Even in the dim light of the remaining street lamps, Joe could see that his face was lightly tanned, although summer was still several months away. He flashed a smile. Joe thought he had too many teeth—and they were too white.

"Hello, Kay," the man said smoothly.

"Hello, Patrick," she replied wearily. "I'm still not interested."

"You haven't even heard Mr. White's latest offer yet."

"I told you before. I've just settled in, and I'm not interested in selling."

The man shook his head slowly. "I don't understand you. We're talking about enough money for you to get a place in a nice, safe area."

Kay sighed. "They don't need what I have to offer in nice, safe areas. This is where I belong, and this is where I'm staying."

"All right," the man replied. "I'll tell Mr. White—but he won't be happy."

The man got back in his car and started the engine. Just before he pulled away he rolled down the window and looked at the Hardys.

"You kids be careful," he said. "You could get hurt around here."

After he drove off Frank turned to Kay Lewis. "What was *that* all about?"

"That was Patrick Smith," she said. "He's the real estate agent who sold me this building. Now he represents a developer named Sam White. It seems Mr. White has taken a sudden interest in this neighborhood, and he's buying up every piece of property he can."

"And you won't sell," Frank said.

Kay nodded. "That's right."

"Maybe this White guy threw that 'cocktail' party earlier to try to scare you off," Joe suggested.

"Maybe we should do some checking around for you," Frank offered.

"I don't want you getting involved in my problems," Kay said. "But thanks anyway."

"Your problem became our problem when that bomb came through the window," Frank replied. "We're in this together now."

The next day after school Frank and Joe drove back to the run-down neighborhood.

"The Scorpions hang out at the video arcade on Becking," Frank said, recalling what Kay Lewis had told them the evening before.

Joe grinned. "So let's go play some games."

"That's exactly what I had in mind," Frank replied as they turned onto Becking Street.

On Becking Street Frank noticed that there weren't as many abandoned buildings as on the block where the self-defense center was located, but most of the structures looked as though they needed some kind of repair—or at least a fresh coat of paint. The arcade was in the middle of the block. It wasn't one of those fancy video-game places like those in malls. It was just a small storefront in an older building.

As they approached the entrance to the arcade Frank noticed two guys leaning against a brick wall, trying to look casual. Frank suspected that they were lookouts.

The two guys eyed the Hardys warily. One of them shot his arm across the entrance, blocking it when Joe tried to walk in.

"Where do you think you're going?" he demanded.

Joe looked at him. "I think I'm going inside—right after I rip your arm off."

Joe started to reach out, but Frank grabbed his sleeve. "Tell Conrad Daye that Frank Hardy wants to talk to him," he said quickly.

"Wait here," the other lookout said. He ducked under his companion's arm and went inside.

A minute later he was back. "Okay, Rad says he'll talk to you."

The one who had blocked the door glared at Joe. "Better watch your mouth," he snarled. "You're on Scorpion territory now."

It took a moment for Joe's eyes to adjust to

the dim light inside. The eerie glow of the video games was about the only source of light. The lookout led them to the back of the arcade, where a lanky guy with shoulder-length brown hair was sitting on an old pinball machine, his legs dangling down, not quite touching the floor.

He was wearing a faded jean jacket with the sleeves torn off. Stitched over the left breast pocket was a small round patch with the likeness of a scorpion on it. In one hand the guy was twirling a butterfly knife, absently flicking the blade in and out of the segmented handle.

He silently studied the Hardys for a moment. Joe realized that the arcade was strangely quiet. In most video-game rooms you had to shout to make yourself heard over the din of electronic sound effects. But not here. Joe didn't have to look around to know that was because nobody was playing any of the games. All eyes were on the two outsiders.

Finally the guy perched on the pinball machine broke the silence. "Hello, Frank," he said coolly. "It's been a long time."

"Hello, Connie," Frank replied.

"You know this guy?" Joe asked, staring at his brother.

"This is Conrad Daye," Frank said. "Connie and I had a few classes together in eighth grade."

The gang leader frowned slightly. "Nobody calls me Connie anymore."

Frank smiled. "Not a very good name for a man in your position, is it?"

Daye grinned and gestured around him with the knife. "We do the best we can with what we've got." The smile faded. "Maybe if my father was an ex-cop and a hotshot detective we'd all be on the football team together. But I had to drop out of school and get a job when my old man hit the road."

Joe stepped forward. He didn't much care for the way Daye talked about the brothers' father, Fenton Hardy. "Is this your idea of a job," he snapped, "joining a gang of punks and rolling old ladies for their pension checks?"

Frank held his breath. The tension in the air was so thick you could cut it with one of the switchblades he heard flicking open behind them.

Conrad Daye eased himself off the pinball machine and fixed his gaze on Joe.

"I hope you didn't have any plans for the rest of the day," the gang leader said coolly, "or for the rest of your life."

Chapter 3

JOE SPUN AROUND and came face-to-face with the gang lookout whose arm he had offered to remove. Except now the guy had eight inches of shining steel clenched in his fist.

The guy shoved the knife up close to Joe's face. "I told you to watch your mouth," he said with a sneer. "Maybe you'll have better manners without a tongue."

Joe jerked his left arm up and knocked the knife out of the way. Then he slammed a quick right jab into the guy's stomach, doubling him over. Joe cocked his arm for a shot to the head, but somebody jumped him from behind.

Two more Scorpions rushed him and grabbed his arms. Joe thrashed around, trying to get loose as they dragged him across the floor and pinned him up against the wall.

"Hold him while I cut him!" a voice growled.

"Back off, Dave!" Conrad Daye shouted. "Everybody, chill out!"

He sounded like a sergeant barking out orders.

Joe just hoped the troops would obey. He could see that Frank was also being held by two of the Scorpions.

"Let them go," Daye said quietly after a moment.

"After what this guy said?"

"We have rules, Dave," the gang leader replied. "We don't do anything that will bring the heat down on us here. The cops would love an excuse to shut this place down.

"Let them go," he repeated firmly.

Joe gave an inward sigh of relief as the hands clutching his arms released him.

Daye turned to Frank. "Take your brother and get out now."

"Sounds reasonable to me," Frank said. He walked over to Joe, took hold of his arm, and hauled him toward the door.

"Oh, one more thing," Daye called out as the Hardys retreated.

Frank turned in the doorway. "What?"

"Now we're even," Daye said.

"What did he mean by that last crack?" Joe asked after they jumped in the van.

Frank turned the key in the ignition, glanced in the side mirror, and pulled away from the curb with a squeal of rubber. "Connie owed me a favor—and you just wasted it."

"Okay, so I got a little out of line," Joe admitted. "But that punk wasn't going to tell us anything."

"He sure wasn't going to tell *you* anything," Frank agreed. "But he might have talked to me."

"Why?"

"Because I helped him out back in junior high. A couple of older guys kept picking on him. They'd shove him around and tell him Connie was a girl's name. They'd keep pushing until he'd get mad and take a swing at one of them. Then they'd beat him up.

"One time," Frank continued, "they made the mistake of razzing him after baseball practice. Daye was carrying his bat—and one of the guys ended up with a couple of cracked ribs and a broken arm."

Frank was quiet for a moment. "I think Daye would have killed him if I hadn't jumped in and stopped it."

"Wait a minute," Joe said. "I think I remember now. Didn't you have to testify in court or something?"

Frank nodded. "The father of the kid with the broken arm tried to get Daye arrested for assault. I was the only witness who wasn't one of the kid's buddies. They all claimed that Daye just started swinging for no reason. I told the police what really happened, and they dropped the charges."

"So that's why he let us get out of there without a scratch," Joe said.

"That's right," said Frank. "But don't expect any more favors from Conrad Daye."

Joe felt pretty stupid for shooting his mouth off in the video arcade. He didn't like gangs. He felt that anybody who joined one was a coward—but he also knew that gangs could be very dangerous. He gazed out the window at the deserted hulk of an old factory. The chain-link fence that blocked the parking lot had a For Sale sign with a Sold sticker plastered over it. There was another sign next to it.

"Pull over a minute," Joe said. He popped open the glove compartment and took out a pencil and a pad of paper.

"What is it?" Frank asked.

Joe nodded toward the sign. "Check it out."

" 'Coming soon,' " Frank read out loud. " 'Another White Development project.' " Below that was a telephone number and an address.

"That must be the developer Kay Lewis mentioned," Joe said as he wrote down the address.

"I guess it's time we paid a visit to Sam White," Frank replied.

The address Joe scribbled on the notepad turned out to be a large hole in the ground just a few blocks away, in the same run-down part of Bayport.

Joe looked out at the deep, muddy pit. "Looks like we're too late," he said. "Somebody's kidnapped Sam White *and* his office."

Frank stopped the van in front of a construction trailer perched on the edge of the pit. The trailer was resting on heavy cinder blocks, and makeshift wooden stairs led to the door. Frank glanced at a sign in front that claimed it was the "Future Site of White Office Plaza."

Frank got out of the van and walked over to the trailer. Joe followed him. Frank climbed the narrow steps and knocked on a small window set in the thin metal door.

"It's open," a voice called from inside. "Come on in."

Frank had to back down the steps to pull open the door. He held it for Joe and then followed him in. The inside of the trailer was one long room. Sitting at a desk at one end was a man with ash gray hair cropped so short Frank could see his scalp.

The man was absorbed in some blueprints spread across the desk. "We're not hiring yet," he said without even looking up. "But if you try again in a few weeks, I may be able to find something for you."

"We're not looking for jobs," Joe said. "We're looking for information."

The man lifted his head and studied the two brothers. His dark, leathery skin told Joe that he spent a lot of time working outside, but the clear, piercing gray eyes set in that rugged face said this was not an ordinary construction worker.

"Sorry," the man said, smiling and sitting back in his chair. "A lot of people walk in off the street looking for work. What can I do for you?"

Joe was direct. "We're looking for Sam White."

The man seemed mildly amused. "And you are . . . ?"

"Frank and Joe Hardy," Frank responded, trying to wrestle control of the conversation from his impatient brother.

The man stood up and walked out from behind the desk. Joe thought he looked like an ex-linebacker—big neck, wide shoulders, muscular arms, and a slightly bulging stomach showing that he had hoisted a few more beers than footballs. The man stuck out his massive right hand.

"Glad to meet you," he said, giving each of them a brief, firm handshake. "I'm Sam White. You'll have to excuse my, ah, office." He gestured to the piles of paper, surveying equipment, and tools that cluttered the trailer. "I'm afraid I can't even offer you a chair."

"That's all right," Frank replied. "We only want to ask you a few questions."

White's thick eyebrows arched. "About what?"

"It looks like you've got big plans for this part of Bayport," Frank said.

White nodded. "That's right. I grew up around here. I figured it was time to give something back to the community."

"Not to mention turn a tidy profit," Joe said casually.

White looked at Joe. "Yes, that, too," he replied evenly. "But I could make money anywhere. Here my projects will bring new homes, new stores, and new jobs to where they're needed most. Do you have a problem with that?"

"So everybody wins," Frank said. "Is that the idea?"

"Yes," White replied. "Something like that." He glanced out the window at the setting sun. "Look, it's getting late, and I've got work to do. So why don't we just get to the point. What exactly is it that you want?"

"We want you to leave Kay Lewis alone," Joe said bluntly.

"What's that supposed to mean?" White snapped. "All I did was offer to buy her building. If that's some kind of crime, it's news to me."

"No, there's no crime in that," Frank agreed. "But somebody tried to burn her alive last night—and that definitely falls on the wrong side of the law, don't you think?"

"Sounds pretty serious," White said calmly. "But what's that got to do with me?"

"We don't know," Frank admitted. "But we plan to find out."

The developer took several brisk strides over to the door, pushed it open, and stood there with his arms crossed. "Like I said before, it's getting late. You'd better get going. It can be dangerous in this neighborhood after dark."

"So can we," Joe replied as he followed his brother out the door.

"Where to now?" Joe asked when they were back in the van again. "Home?"

Frank shrugged. "I don't know. So far we haven't found out anything we didn't know last night. White admits that he wants Kay's property —but that's all we have on him." He stared out the windshield for a moment, lost in thought. "Tell you what," he said at last. "Let's see if Kay can tell us anything more."

"Might as well," Joe replied. "We're already in the neighborhood."

Frank peered down the street. "Let's see. If we take a left up at the next light, that should take us right to Madison."

Joe nodded. "And since the self-defense school is on Madison, that's right where we want to be."

Frank put the van in gear and then flicked on the headlights. Sam White had been right about one thing—it was getting late. Trying to conduct an investigation after school could really put a cramp in your style.

As they turned onto Madison Frank saw the Bayport Savings Bank, where Chet Morton worked part-time. It was an older building, without a drive-through banking center. Most of the lights were out, and Frank guessed the bank was closed for the day.

"Hey," Joe said, pointing out the window. "Isn't that Chet's car?"

Frank was just starting to turn his head when Joe suddenly clutched at his arm and yelled, "Stop the van!"

Frank slammed on the brakes. The van swerved and screeched to a halt. "What is it?" he shouted. But he could already see the answer for himself.

Framed in the headlights, a body lay sprawled facedown on the ground. And spreading slowly across the pavement was a dark pool of blood.

Chapter 4

Joe bolted out of the van before it stopped moving. Kneeling beside the body, he could see that it was Chet Morton. On his forehead was an ugly gash, which was the source of all the blood on the pavement. But Joe could tell that the wound wasn't deep and that the bleeding had almost stopped already.

Joe carefully rolled his friend over onto his back. Chet's eyes fluttered open. "Ooh," he moaned. "My head feels like somebody dropped an anvil on it." He sat up slowly, holding on to Joe's arm for support. "I could've taken them, Joe—but one of them blindsided me."

"Who?" Joe asked. "Who did this to you?"

Chet tried to shake his head and winced in pain. "I don't know. They were wearing ski masks."

Frank appeared next to his brother. "I found a pay phone and called an ambulance." He bent down next to Chet. "What happened?"

"I left my gym bag at the self-defense center

yesterday," Chet said. "I went over there after work to pick it up. On the way back to my car three guys jumped me."

"How much money did they get?" Joe asked.

"That's the weird part," Chet answered. "They didn't try to rob me. One of them mumbled something about wimps who need women to protect them, and then they were all over me. I got a few good licks in, though. One of them is going to need major dental work."

"Anything at all that might identify them?" Frank asked.

"No," Chet replied. "Nothing that I can think of, anyway. It all happened pretty fast. I think I'm okay now—unless they did something to the car. If anything happened to the car, my mother will kill me."

Frank went over to Chet's car and took a close look. "Seems all right to me," he said. "Not a scratch on—" He stopped in midsentence. A glint of metal in the narrow space between the front tire and the curb caught his eye. He bent down to get a closer look. Then he carefully picked up the metal object, holding one end lightly between the tips of his forefinger and thumb. He didn't want to get any fingerprints on it.

Joe glanced over at his brother. "What've you got there?"

Frank showed it to him. "A balisong."

Chet Morton frowned. "A what song?"

"A butterfly knife," Frank explained. "Kind of the martial-arts answer to the switchblade."

Joe stood up and took a closer look. "Wasn't Conrad Daye fiddling around with one of those in the video arcade?"

Frank nodded and started to open his mouth to respond to Joe. But before he could say anything he heard the wail of a siren.

"Sounds like an ambulance," Joe said.

"And the police won't be too far behind," Frank replied.

Joe grinned halfheartedly. "Gee, I bet they'll be glad to see us again."

"I still don't get it," Joe complained, tossing his books in his locker and swinging the metal door shut with a resounding clank. "Why didn't you give the knife to the police yesterday?"

Frank shrugged as they jostled through the crowded hallway. Every day at the exact stroke of 3:00 Bayport High emptied out faster than it had for any fire drill in the school's history.

"It doesn't prove anything," Frank said. "Anybody could get a knife like that."

"But it's evidence in a criminal investigation," Joe argued. He felt more than a little weird reminding Frank about proper procedure. Usually it was Joe who wanted to throw away the rule book and fake it.

The crowd spilled out the front entrance of the school and spread in all directions. Frank and

Joe headed for the parking lot. "I know," Frank said uneasily. "It just seems a little too convenient."

"How so?" Joe asked. He stuck his hand in his front pocket, fished out the keys to the van, and unlocked the door.

"Well," Frank said as he climbed into the passenger seat, "don't you think it's kind of strange that we find a knife just like Daye's at the scene of a crime an hour after we talk to him?"

"Yeah, I guess so," Joe admitted. "So what do you want to do now?"

"Have another talk with Conrad Daye," Frank said.

Joe looked at his brother. "After what happened yesterday?"

Frank smiled. "Don't worry—I've got a plan."

"That's when I worry the most," Joe replied. "What is it this time?"

"I'll keep quiet while you drive," Frank said, "and you keep quiet while I talk to Daye."

"Pull over here," Frank told Joe when they got to Becking Street.

Joe looked down the street. The video arcade was a little over a block away. He could see two or three empty parking spaces right in front of the gang hangout. "Trying to save gas?" he ventured. "Or are we going to walk the rest of the way because it's good exercise?"

"I'm not in a real big hurry to jump in there again," Frank answered. "And sooner or later Daye has to come out. So why don't we wait a while and see if we get lucky?"

"We don't even know if he's in there," Joe pointed out.

"That's true," Frank agreed. "So why risk our lives taking on the rest of the gang if the guy we want isn't even there?"

"Good point," Joe said. "Hey—I've got an idea."

"What?"

"Let's wait here and see if we get lucky."

"Good plan," Frank said.

They didn't have to wait very long. About a half hour later Conrad Daye came out of the arcade—but he wasn't alone.

"That's the guy who wanted my tongue for his trophy case," Joe growled.

Frank nodded. "Yeah—Dave somebody. I didn't catch his last name."

Joe started to open the van door. "He won't even remember his last name when I get through with him."

Frank grabbed Joe's shirt sleeve and yanked him back into his seat. "You're not going to do anything, remember?"

Joe knew his brother was right. "Okay," he grumbled.

"Get ready," Frank said. "Here they come."

The Hardys waited until the two gang members had passed the van. Then they slipped out and followed them down the street.

Frank quietly walked up behind Conrad Daye. "Hello, Connie," he said casually.

Daye whirled around. "What th—" he began. He stopped himself when he saw Frank and Joe. "You guys just won't take a hint," he said angrily.

"Don't waste your breath talking to these zeros," his companion sneered.

Dave reached into his pocket, but Joe closed in on him and grabbed his arm before he could pull out the switchblade. Then Joe grasped Dave's right hand and pumped it up and down. "Hi," he said, grinning. "I'm Joe Hardy. I don't think we've been properly introduced."

"Better tell him your name before he shakes your arm out of the socket," Conrad Daye suggested.

"Dave Gilson."

Joe released his crushing grip and clapped Gilson on the shoulder. "That's more like it! I feel much better now. Don't you?"

Gilson just stared at him.

"All right," Daye said, turning to Frank. "You've got me. Now what do you want?"

"I hear you've got a problem with the new self-defense school over on Madison," Frank said. "Is that true?"

"What kind of problem?" the gang leader responded. "If a bunch of girls and wimps want to throw their money away, that's their problem, not mine."

"But it's on your turf," Frank said. "That doesn't bother you?"

"Sure," Daye admitted. "A lot of things bother me. So what?"

"Somebody threw a firebomb into the school the other day," Frank answered. "And after we came to see you yesterday, somebody jumped a friend of ours near there."

"And you think the Scorpions did it?" Daye asked sharply.

"I don't know what to think," Frank said honestly. "But the evidence seems to point in that direction."

"What evidence?"

Frank pulled a clear plastic bag out of his pocket. In it was the knife he had found next to Chet Morton's car. "Look familiar?"

Daye was silent for a moment. "That doesn't prove anything," he said. There was a slight edge in his voice. "A lot of guys have knives like that."

"Yeah," Frank replied. "That's what I said, too. Of course, there's one easy way to settle the whole thing. Just show me your knife. If you still have it, then this can't be it. Right?"

Daye glared at Frank. "You're not a cop. I don't have to prove anything to you."

"We don't have to take this!" Gilson cut in. "Come on, Rad. Let's get going."

"No," Daye replied. "I want to settle this now." He looked at Frank. "You said somebody took down your friend yesterday after you came by the arcade, right?"

Frank nodded.

"I never left the arcade," Daye continued. "I was there all evening—and I've got a dozen witnesses."

"I've had enough of this," Gilson said. He shouldered his way past Joe and walked away. "I'm out of here."

"Gee, that's too bad," Joe said. "He was just starting to grow on me—like fungus."

Daye followed his friend. "Just drop it, Frank," he said over his shoulder.

"You know I can't do that," Frank replied. But Daye was already gone.

"Nice alibi," Joe said. "His twelve 'witnesses' would swear he was on Pluto at the time, if that's what he told them to say."

"We should still check it out," Frank responded. "But I want to see Kay Lewis first."

"That's what you said yesterday," Joe reminded him. "It seems like every time we go near her place somebody gets hurt."

It was just a short drive to the self-defense center. As the Hardys got out of the van Kay Lewis walked out the front door. She had a stack of envelopes in one hand and was trying to lock the door with the other.

Joe jogged over and grabbed the letters just before they tumbled to the ground.

"Thanks," she said. "But I hope you guys didn't drive all this way to see me. I'm in a bit of a hurry. I have to get to the post office before five."

Joe grinned and gestured to the van. "Your limousine awaits."

"Thanks for the offer," she replied, "but I've got my own car."

"Well, then," Frank said, "we'll walk you to your car."

"It'll be a pretty short walk," she said, pointing to the alley next to the building. "It's parked right over there."

"In the alley?" Joe responded.

Kay let out a short laugh. "Around here, that's the safest place—even the muggers are afraid of the alleys.

"I heard about Chet," she said, shifting to a serious tone. "The local punks have given some of my students a hard time, but they've never attacked anybody. Do you think it's connected to the firebombing and the letters?"

"It might be," Frank answered. "We were hoping that you could tell us something that might help."

Kay shrugged. "I don't know what—but feel free to ask anything you want anytime. Anytime but now," she added as she unlocked the car door and slid into the driver's seat. "I've really got to go."

"No problem," Frank said. "We'll drop by later."

As the Hardys walked back to the van Kay Lewis drove up next to them and rolled down the car window. "I'll be back in about an hour," she told them.

"Great," Frank said. "We'll see you then."

As she started to pull away Joe spotted a white envelope lying on the sidewalk. "Wait!" he shouted, scooping up the letter and running after the car.

Kay stopped her car, got out, and walked back toward Joe. "What's wrong?" she asked.

"You must have dropped this," Joe explained.

She looked at the letter in his hand. "Oh, thanks. That was—"

Her words were cut off by a thunderous explosion and a searing flash of light.

Frank saw the blast rip apart Kay's car. He shielded his head with his hands as chunks of flaming metal rained down on him. And he saw Kay and his brother lifted off the ground by the explosive force of the blast and hurled through the air like lifeless rag dolls.

Chapter 5

FRANK RAN toward his brother, ignoring the intense heat. Kay Lewis was on her hands and knees, struggling to stand—but Joe wasn't moving. Frank clutched Joe's shoulders and dragged him away from the blazing wreckage.

Joe stared up at his brother. He tried to say something, but he couldn't get any air in his lungs. That spooked him, and he tried to yell. That just made it worse.

"Relax, Joe," Frank said firmly. "You got the wind knocked out of you. Just relax and you'll be able to breathe again."

Joe closed his eyes and forced himself to count. One . . . two . . . three . . . Gradually the stranglehold on his lungs loosened its grip. Fresh air started to work its way into his system. "Help me stand up," he gasped, grasping Frank's forearm.

When Joe was on his feet he turned to Kay Lewis. "You should have somebody look at that engine," engine," he wheezed. "That sucker needs a tune-up."

* * *

For a while it seemed as if every squad car in Bayport was crawling around the blackened heap of Kay Lewis's car. "They're either going to throw it in the slammer,"Joe whispered to Frank, "or they're going to have a cookout."

Even Police Chief Collig was there—and he wasn't very happy. "You seem to be the center of a lot of unusual activity," he sourly told the boys.

Joe shrugged. "We're sort of gifted that way, I guess."

The police chief wasn't amused. "I'll give you a gift, Joe. I won't hold you as a material witness to attempted murder if you tell me what's going on here."

"We don't know much more than you do," Frank replied. "What about the car?"

Collig glanced at the charred wreckage. "It's too soon to tell for sure, but it looks like plastic explosives wired to the ignition. It was probably set to detonate when the engine started." He shifted his gaze to Kay Lewis, "Luckily, they didn't do a very good job.

"Are you sure you don't know who did this?" he asked, turning back to Frank.

"Absolutely," Frank said quickly. It was the truth. He didn't know—he only had suspects.

The police chief sighed and walked away, shaking his head.

Joe leaned over and whispered to his brother, "What about the knife?"

Frank answered with a question. "Where do you think a bunch of street punks like the Scorpions could get their hands on plastic explosives—*and* learn how to use them?"

"From a new video game?" Joe ventured lamely.

"Just for the moment," Frank replied, "let's assume that's not very likely. Now, who would have easy access to explosives of all kinds and the experience to wire them?"

Joe thought about it for a moment. "A demolitions expert. Somebody who blows up old buildings."

"Right," Frank said. "Somebody who blows up old buildings *and* puts up new ones."

Joe felt like an idiot for not thinking of it himself. "Sam White."

"And who can tell us more about the developer with big plans?" Frank asked.

"That real estate agent—what was his name?"

"Patrick Smith," Kay Lewis answered.

"Then I guess we go see Patrick Smith," Joe concluded.

Smith's office was in a shiny glass-and-chrome building surrounded by manicured lawns, automatic sprinklers, and a security system right out of a high-tech spy movie. Frank pressed the buzzer with Smith's name on it while Joe made faces at the video surveillance camera.

"Who is it?" a tinny man's voice crackled over the intercom.

"Frank and Joe Hardy," Frank answered.

"Who?"

Frank leaned over and spoke directly into the microphone. "We were with Kay Lewis the other night when you dropped by."

"Sure, I remember," came the reply. "Come on up. Third floor, first office on the right."

There was a harsh electronic buzz and a loud click, and then the door swung open. Frank and Joe went in, found the elevator, and rode up to the third floor.

Patrick Smith was waiting for them at the door to his office. "Something tells me you aren't here to buy a house," he said, ushering them inside. "So take a seat and tell me what's on your mind."

"I hope we're not interrupting anything," Frank said. "I know it's kind of late. We weren't even sure you'd be here."

"My workday never ends," the realtor responded. "I showed a house to a customer this evening and came back to the office to finish up some paperwork. Some days I work fifteen hours or more. My secretary, however, doesn't share my enthusiasm for the real estate business. A minute after five she's nowhere in sight."

Frank noticed a computer on the desk. It was

connected to a telephone modem. "Nice," he said. "I bet you get instant information on all the property for sale in Bayport with that."

Smith flashed a salesman's smile and patted the top of the computer. "That's right. I can even access public records on property taxes, land surveys, building plans. You name it."

"Is that legal?" Joe asked.

"Yep," Smith replied. "The realtors' association maintains a data base of property listings for all its members, and the city provides electronic access to all building information available to the general public. It makes my job pretty easy."

"So," Frank said, "if I wanted a list of all the properties owned by a certain company, you could just call it up on the screen."

"A certain company," Smith repeated. "Like White Development, for instance? I heard about your little visit with Sam White."

"I thought you might," Frank replied. "You do a lot of work for him, right?"

"He buys and sells a lot of buildings," Smith answered. "And that's how I make my living."

"Why does he want Kay Lewis's place?" Joe asked. "And how far do you think he'd go to get it?"

"Kay Lewis moved into a dangerous part of town," Smith replied. "Now she's paying the price. If I were you, I wouldn't waste a lot of time looking for complex conspiracies."

"But you're not us," Frank said evenly.

"And Sam White doesn't pay our rent," Joe added.

The realtor looked at Joe. "Sam White is an important client—but if I thought he was doing anything illegal, I'd call the police and report it." He glanced down at his computer and started tapping something on the keyboard. "Come here, let me show you something."

Frank and Joe walked around to where they could see the computer screen. Smith tapped a few more keys and then sat back in his chair. The computer hummed quietly to itself. After a few seconds something that looked like a schematic drawing or a blueprint popped up on the color monitor.

"These are the plans for a shopping mall," Smith explained. "Sam White plans to build it across the street from where the self-defense school is now."

"Across the street?" Joe asked.

"That's right," Smith said. "With or without Kay Lewis's property, the mall will get built. White just wants the land on the other side of the street for extra parking."

He tapped another key, and the image blinked off the screen. "So you see, Sam White doesn't really need her property—and I doubt that he even wants it enough to try to scare her off. If he can't buy it the good old-fashioned way, he'll just go ahead and build the mall without the additional parking space."

Smith sat back in his chair, his hands clasped behind his head. "Does that answer your questions?"

Frank studied Smith, but the realtor's expression never changed. The smile pasted on his face never faded, so it was impossible to tell if he was lying.

Smith was a salesman, and he was doing a sales job on them. Frank had no doubt about that. "Yes," he replied coolly. "I think that pretty much covers everything." He turned to his brother. "Don't you, Joe?"

"Ah, sure," Joe agreed. He knew what Frank really meant was "Let's get out of here now."

Later that night at home, long after their parents had gone to bed, Frank was still hunched over the computer—and Joe was leaning over his shoulder.

It was easy getting into the Bayport City Hall computer files. They had done it lots of times before, and as Patrick Smith had said, it was all perfectly legal.

But you have to know what you're looking for, Frank reminded himself—and you have to know the name of the file it's buried in.

He knew what he was looking for—any information on 2515 Madison, the building owned by Kay Lewis. But finding it in the thousands of electronic files was a little trickier.

Frank's fingers were a blur on the keyboard.

File directory names scrolled up the monitor screen. If he saw one that sounded good, he checked it out. After a while he had to glance only at the first few entries in a directory to know it was a dead end.

Finally his fingers stopped moving, his hands dropped off the keyboard, and he slumped back in his chair.

"You're not giving up, are you?" Joe protested.

Frank shook his head slowly. There was a smile on his face. "Check it out," he said.

Joe looked at the monitor. At the top of the screen the address of Kay's building appeared in bold type.

"This file," Frank explained, "will tell us when it was built, who built it, and everyone who's ever owned it. See? There's Kay's name at the top, under 'current owner.' "

Joe scanned the dates and names on the screen. "It sure has gone through a lot of different hands," he noted.

"Look at the dates," Frank said. "Most of those are in the last ten years, after that area hit the skids. But if you go back further, you can see—"

Frank stopped in midsentence, absorbed in something he had found in the computer file.

"See what?" Joe prodded.

"Jake Barton," Frank said, pointing at one of the entries.

Joe grinned. "Now, there's a piece of local

history. Bayport's own Al Capone clone. A genuine tommy-gun-totin', cigar-chompin' gangster. If Barracuda Barton used to live there, Kay could get that pile of bricks declared a historical landmark."

"The time frame fits," Frank remarked. "According to this, he bought the building in 1923 and sold it in 1929."

"Maybe there's a secret vault filled with gold," Joe suggested hopefully.

"Yeah, right," Frank replied, "and Barton forgot all about it when he moved out. And it's just been sitting down there all these years, waiting for us to find it."

"Okay," Joe said glumly, "it was a stupid idea. So what does any of this information tell us?"

"Beats me," Frank said. "But let's get a printout of it anyway." He typed in a command, and the printer obediently started chattering away.

When the printer stopped, Frank turned off the computer. At the same instant the phone rang. Shutting down the computer also switched off the modem. It was just like hanging up the phone. The caller might have been trying to get through for hours.

"Must be important," Joe said as he reached for the receiver. "This better be good," he spoke into the phone. "It's very late, and I need my beauty rest."

"There's a package waiting for you in the

alley next to the self-defense center,'' a muffled voice said over the line. ''But you'd better hurry and get it before it's too late.''

''Who is this?'' Joe demanded. ''Too late for what?'' But the only answer he got was a click and the drone of the dial tone.

Chapter 6

JOE HUNG UP the phone and told Frank what he had just heard. "It could be a trap," he added.

Frank nodded. "But we've got to check it out anyway."

Joe sighed. "Somehow I just knew you were going to say that."

They silently sneaked downstairs so their parents wouldn't hear them, and they slipped out the front door. Frank climbed into the driver's seat of the van, pushed the shift into neutral, and popped the emergency brake.

Standing in front of the van, Joe put his shoulder to the grille and gave a solid shove. Then he ran around the side and jumped in as the van started to roll back down the gently sloping driveway.

Frank didn't start the engine until they hit the street, and he didn't turn on the headlights until they were a block from home.

Half a block from the self-defense center Frank

cut the lights, killed the engine, and let the dark van coast down the deserted street. He angled over toward the curb and lightly stepped on the brake pedal. The van silently rolled to a stop.

Frank and Joe slipped out and padded down the street, darting quickly past the dirty yellow glow of a lone streetlight.

Frank put his hand out and waved Joe to a halt at the mouth of the dark alley. He peered around the corner, trying to penetrate the gloom. He could make out the lurking shapes of a few trash cans—and then he caught a glimmer of movement. "Looks like we've got company," he whispered to his brother.

Joe responded by standing up straight, flipping up the collar of his jacket, and casually strolling past the alley to the building on the other side. Then he swiftly flattened himself against the wall and nodded to Frank.

Frank wasn't exactly thrilled with his brother's improvised "plan"—but there was no stopping Joe once he got an idea into his head. Frank took a deep breath and plunged into the darkness, knowing Joe would follow his lead.

Frank had barely entered the alley when a shape rushed toward him. Without thinking, Frank struck out with an open-hand blow aimed at where he thought his attacker's face should be. He channeled the force of his forward momentum into the blow, just as he had learned in karate school.

There was a blur of motion, and something slapped against his inner forearm, deflecting the blow. A classic circular block, Frank realized too late. Then a hard fist connected with Frank's stomach. He fought the urge to bend into the pain. Sensing the direction of the next strike, he snapped his head back.

There was a piercing yell of "Ki-ya!" as a palm-heel blow grazed the bottom of Frank's chin.

Joe was circling around to come in from behind when the attacker's sudden yell startled him. He thought he recognized the voice. "Kay?" he called out.

All the shadowy movement in the alley froze. "Move out into the light where I can see you," a female voice ordered.

Joe and Frank backed out of the alley slowly. "You see?" Joe said, turning his face toward the street light. "It's just us—the lovable Hardy brothers."

Kay Lewis stepped out of the gloom. "What are you doing here?" she demanded. She turned to Frank. "I could have killed you."

Frank ran his hand along his bruised chin. "I don't doubt it," he said. He knew the full force of the upward palm-heel thrust could have shattered his jaw. Kay Lewis was one tough lady.

"We got a phone call," Joe explained. "Something about some kind of package in the alley."

"You, too?" Kay replied. "That's why I was out here."

Frank smiled. "That's a relief. For a minute I thought maybe you practiced your self-defense moves by hanging out in dark alleys, waiting for unsuspecting muggers."

Kay chuckled. "Well, now that we're all here, we might as well look for whatever it is we're supposed to find."

Frank pulled out a pocket-size flashlight and flicked on its high-intensity beam. "Let's do it," he said.

The search didn't take long. After all, Frank reminded himself, somebody *wanted* them to find the package. It was about the size of a shoe box, wrapped in brown paper. Frank handed the flashlight to Joe and picked up the package. He carefully removed the wrapping and uncovered . . . a shoe box.

"Terrific," Joe muttered. "We've stumbled onto an international ring of shoe thieves."

Frank put one hand on the lid and turned the box over slowly, making sure the lid stayed firmly in place. "Give me your pocketknife," he said to Joe. "I'm going to cut open the bottom and get a look at what's inside."

"Wouldn't it be easier just to take off the lid?" Kay Lewis asked.

"Not if it's booby-trapped," Frank replied. He took Joe's knife and made a small cut in the box. "Now shine the light down here," he told his brother as he lifted up the flap he had sliced in the cardboard.

Inside the box was a grayish lump of something that looked like modeling clay with a shiny coating. Frank gently placed the shoe box on the ground. "I think I've seen enough," he said in a low voice. "It's time to call the cops."

"Not again!" Joe groaned. "What's in there that we can't handle ourselves?"

"Plastic explosives," Frank answered.

"Oh," Joe said, eyeing the box warily. "Hey, I've got an idea."

"What?" Frank responded.

Joe smiled weakly. "Let's call the cops."

"I've got a better idea," Kay said. "I'll call the cops while you two get out of here. I don't think Chief Collig would be real happy to see your faces right now."

"Sooner or later we'll have to tell him we were here," Frank said.

"Then let it be later," Kay urged. "Come back tomorrow, and I'll let you know what happened."

Joe nodded. "I'm too tired to play twenty questions with Collig right now. Let's deal with it tomorrow."

Reluctantly, Frank agreed, and they went home. But neither of them got much sleep.

No one in uniform marched into Bayport High and hauled the Hardys away in the middle of the day, but Joe kept hoping. Intense police interrogation had to be better than the essay test he was forced to endure. When the school day finally ended and Frank and Joe headed for the van, somebody else was already there waiting for them.

"Hi, guys," Callie Shaw said. "I decided the best way to find you was to stake out your wheels."

She turned to Frank. "I haven't seen much of you the last couple of days."

"Sorry," Frank said. "I guess we got kind of wrapped up in this case."

"That's what I figured," she replied. "And since I got you into this thing in the first place, I want to help."

"How about going home and leaving us alone?" Joe suggested. "That would be a big help."

Callie looked at Joe. "Either we all go together in the van, or I follow you around in my car. Either way, wherever you go, I go."

"We all go together," Frank declared before Joe could say anything else.

Joe shrugged and opened the van door. "Ladies first," he said with a smile. If she had to come along, at least he was going to make sure she got stuck in the middle and he got the window seat.

They drove straight to the AAA Self-defense Center to meet with Kay Lewis.

"Are there any quadruple-A self-defense centers?" Joe wondered out loud as he looked at the sign. "Just how good is a triple-A rating anyway?"

"It's not a rating," Callie explained as they stepped out of the van. "It stands for attitude, awareness, and assertion. Kay says you have to believe that you can defend yourself. You should visualize yourself surviving the attack before the first blow is struck. That's the attitude part.

"You should also be aware of the situation," Callie continued. "If you can read your opponent's physical and verbal cues, you can stay one step ahead."

Callie slipped in between Frank and Joe as they walked up the front steps. "But the real key to self-defense," she said, reaching out and rapping on the door, "is to assert yourself. Take control of the situation. Don't be overly aggressive—and don't be a victim."

"So you've asserted yourself against a vicious, trained attack door," Joe remarked. "What happens if nobody answers?"

"You try the knob," Frank replied, turning the doorknob and pushing the door open. "And become aware that it is unlocked."

Frank poked his head inside. "Hello?" he shouted. "Anybody home?"

"Nobody here but rats and mildew!" a muted voice responded.

"Where are you?" Frank called out.

"In the basement," the voice replied. "Come on down."

They found the door to the basement and climbed down the steep wooden stairs.

"Watch your head," Joe heard somebody say—just as his forehead smacked into a support beam running along the low ceiling.

Joe staggered forward, more stunned than hurt. A pair of hands reached out to steady him, and Joe found himself staring at Con Riley.

"Just the fellows I was looking for," Riley said.

Kay Lewis was standing off to one side, holding a large box in both hands. "You guys are just in time," she said.

"Time for what?" Joe asked nervously.

Kay smiled. "You're just in time to help me move these boxes. But first you might want to hear what the police found out about my 'special delivery' last night."

Riley looked at the Hardys. "I don't know why I should tell you any of this. You're already on Chief Collig's hit list. You're just lucky Ms. Lewis told me everything last night so I could run interference for you today."

"What was in the box?" Frank asked. "Was it plastic explosive?"

The police officer nodded. "And we lifted a couple of clean sets of fingerprints off the box."

"One of them was probably mine," Frank said. "Did you get a make on the others?"

"We fed them into the computer," Riley replied, "and got a match in about thirty seconds, right out of our local files."

"Don't tell me," Joe cut in. "Let me guess."

"Conrad Daye," Frank said grimly.

Con Riley nodded again.

Joe looked at his brother. "I told you not to tell me."

Frank didn't hear him. He was turning something over in his mind. Finally, he came to a decision. He reached into his front pants pocket and pulled out the plastic bag with the knife inside.

"Here," he said, handing it to Con Riley. "I found this near the spot where Chet Morton was attacked. You'll probably find Daye's prints all over it, too."

Riley studied the knife and then jotted something in his notepad. "If you're right, together with what we already have," he said, "this should give us enough evidence to put him away for a long time."

The police officer gave Frank a stern look. "You should have turned in the knife when you found it. That car bomb the other day almost killed your brother. Maybe some of this could have been prevented if you had just let the police do their job."

"Maybe," Frank replied. "But I doubt it."

Chapter 7

AFTER CON RILEY LEFT, Frank slumped down on the stairs and brooded.

Kay Lewis glanced at him and then turned to Joe. "Is he always this happy when a case is over?"

"I don't know," Joe said. "I'll ask him. Hey, Frank, are you always this happy when a case is over?"

"What makes you think it's over?" Frank asked.

Callie walked over and touched his arm lightly. "What's the matter? The police have an APB out for Conrad Daye. As soon as they catch him that'll be the end of it—and you found the evidence they need to put him away."

"Maybe that's what's bothering me," Frank said. "We didn't find the evidence—it was practically handed to us."

Joe shrugged. "Maybe somebody else in his gang thought he'd gone too far or wanted to take over. So he decided to help us out a little." Joe knew that the whole thing had "setup" written all over it—but that didn't mean Daye wasn't guilty. It just meant one of his buddies had rolled over on him. Joe didn't believe in honor among thieves, and neither did Frank . . . usually.

Joe shook his head. He liked to keep things simple. "Did you know that Jake Barton once lived here?" he said, changing the subject.

"The name sounds familiar," Kay replied, "but I can't place it."

"He's kind of a Bayport legend," Joe said. "He was a gangster way back in the Roaring Twenties. He might even have used this place as his headquarters."

"Of course!" Kay exclaimed. "That explains it!"

"Explains what?" Callie asked.

"Follow me," Kay answered, "and I'll show you."

She walked toward a door at the far end of the basement. At one time somebody had tried to liven up the cramped, damp, windowless room by slapping a coat of white paint on the walls. Out of zeal the person had also painted the door.

Upon closer inspection Joe could tell that the door was made of solid steel. The door frame set in the brick wall was steel, too. Joe ran his hand over the door's cold metal surface. He touched the lever-style door handle. The latch mechanism was on the door itself. Flat metal bars connected the handle to steel rods that were placed horizontally across the top and bottom of the door. The rods went through the door frame into the brick wall.

"Crude—but effective," Frank said from over Joe's shoulder. "No lock to pick. No weak spots for a forced entry. Anybody on the other side would have a real tough time getting through that."

"What's on the other side?" Joe asked. "A two-thousand-pound man-eating gorilla?"

"Open it and see," Kay said.

Joe pushed down on the lever, and the steel bolts pulled free from their anchors in the wall. He gripped the handle tightly and gave it a good, solid tug. The door creaked open to reveal . . . another steel door. It looked just like the one Joe had just opened, except this one didn't have a handle or any visible latch.

"Cute," Joe said. "What now?"

"Push it," Kay told him. "It's not locked."

Joe put his weight against the door—and almost fell on his face when it swung inward easily. He stumbled forward and found himself in a small room with brick walls and a concrete floor. The back wall was lined with empty wooden shelves covered with a thick layer of brick dust.

Frank, Callie, and Kay followed him in. Frank quickly glanced around the chamber and then turned to take a closer look at the second door. "Check this out, Joe," he said. "It's a mirror image of the first door. It's got the same latch mechanism on the inside of the other room."

Joe frowned. "I don't get it. How could anybody ever pass from one room to the other?"

"Think of it as a two-part manual security system," Frank replied.

Joe closed his eyes. "Okay, I'm thinking." He opened his eyes again. "I still don't get it."

"There had to be a guard or somebody on both sides for anybody to get in or out," Frank explained.

"Then how did we manage it?" Callie asked.

"Somebody bypassed the security system," Frank said, pointing to the lever-style handle of the second door. It was held down in the open position by a length of wire wrapped around it and tied to the flat metal bar beneath it.

"And you laughed when I talked about a secret vault," Joe said smugly.

"It was the part about the gold that cracked me up," Frank replied.

"Well, he *could* have stashed his loot down here," Joe persisted.

Frank nodded toward the rusted-out remains of a potbellied stove in one corner. "Yeah, he could have—but why would he need a *heated* vault? My guess is that this is where they kept the books."

"Books?" Kay asked. "What kind of books?"

"A big criminal organization keeps records just like a big corporation," Frank said. "They have to keep track of what they have, who owes them money—"

"Whose legs need breaking," Joe chimed in.

"That, too," Frank agreed. "And that's why somebody like Jake Barton would have kept his books in a guarded, concealed spot like this—because those records were evidence of illegal activity.

"So he sealed off part of the basement and stuck his bookkeepers underground," Frank went on. "The stove wasn't for heat—it was for burning the books if there was a raid. By the time the police managed to break down the door, the evidence would be a cloud of smoke."

"It all fits," Kay remarked, "except for the part about sealing off the basement."

"What would you call it?" Joe responded.

"I'd call it adding on," Kay said. "Because the basement ends there." She pointed to the brick wall with the steel door. "They cut a hole through the foundation wall and carved this chamber out of the ground."

Callie looked up. "Then what's above us?"

"As far as I can tell," Kay answered, "several feet of dirt."

Joe started to feel crowded in the confined space. A secret vault filled with buried treasure was one thing. A clandestine accounting office was quite another. In fact, it was *boring*.

"Whoa! Look at the time," he said, barely glancing at his watch. "We'd better get going.

Come on, guys.'' Joe hustled Frank and Callie out of the room and back upstairs to the van.

They dropped Callie off at her house, and Frank hardly said a word the rest of the way home. He was thinking about the ''addition'' to Kay's basement. There was something about it that didn't quite mesh—but he couldn't put his finger on it.

As soon as they got home Frank headed straight for the computer and the printout he had run off the day before. He skimmed through the small stack of paper and found what he was looking for.

''What've you got there?'' Joe asked.

Frank showed him a computerized building plan. ''This is a schematic of Kay's building,'' he said.

''So?'' Joe responded. ''I doubt if Jake Barton filed a building plan with the city when he decided to knock a hole in the foundation.''

''No,'' Frank said, tapping the paper, ''but it's here anyway.''

Joe looked at his brother. ''Care to explain that one to me?''

''Somebody probably did some renovation on the place after Barton was long gone,'' Frank answered. ''When that happens, the city sends an inspector to check out the structure and okay the building permit. The inspector noticed the extra room off the basement and filed a revised plan."

Frank sat down and studied the printout. "Everything's here. Plumbing fixtures, electrical wiring, heating pipes—the works."

"Let me see," Joe said, crowding in next to Frank to get a better look. "Oh, yeah. Here's the furnace, and the exhaust vent through the chimney—"

"Exhaust vent," Frank said, cutting him off. "That's it. That's what's wrong."

A puzzled look crossed Joe's face. "What's wrong with the exhaust vent?"

"Remember the potbellied stove?" Frank replied.

Joe nodded.

"The smokestack went into the outside wall," Frank said. "But there's nothing like that on this plan."

Joe shrugged. "So they missed a detail."

Frank picked up the paper and waved it in his brother's face. "That's not the point! Where does the pipe go? The whole room is underground."

"Wait a minute," Joe said. "You can't vent smoke into the ground."

"Right," Frank replied. "There's got to be something on the other side of that wall."

The two brothers looked at each other. They both knew they couldn't wait another day to find out.

"It's almost dinnertime," Joe pointed out.

"I'm not hungry," Frank said.

Joe grinned. "I am—but I'll survive. Let's go." He raced Frank downstairs and out to the van.

Joe didn't pay much attention to the pair of headlights that winked on down the block as he backed the van out of the driveway. But after a few minutes he began to worry. Every time he turned, the headlights followed. "Take a look in the side mirror," he told Frank. "Looks like we've grown a tail."

Frank glanced in the mirror. "Well, let's try to wag it and see what happens."

"Hang on," Joe replied, punching the gas pedal.

The van lurched forward, gaining speed. Without taking his foot off the gas Joe suddenly cranked the wheel hard to the right, screeching onto a dimly lit side street. His eyes darted to the side mirror. He heard the squeal of rubber and saw the headlights coming around the corner. Joe had pulled a little ahead with his surprise move, but now the headlights were growing larger in the mirror, closing the gap.

Joe hung a tight left. The van rocked violently and almost flipped over. Joe wrestled the wheel. Another check of the mirror told him the headlights were still there—even closer than before. At the next side street Joe started to turn again.

"No!" Frank shouted. "Not down here!"

The glare of the van's lights glinted off the

Dead End sign. Joe slammed on the brakes, yanking hard on the wheel at the same time. The van swerved, spun around, and stopped. Joe was ready to gun the van and blast it back out of the cul-de-sac.

But there was no place to go. The headlights were already there, glaring right at them, blocking the only way out.

Chapter 8

JOE'S EYES NARROWED, and he revved the engine. "I hope that guy's got a good insurance policy—because he's going to need it."

Frank glanced at his brother. "What are you going to do—try to drive through him?"

"You got a better idea?" Joe responded.

Frank squinted through the windshield, trying to see past the bright headlights. "Yeah. Let's find out what he wants. Look—somebody's getting out."

A tall figure with long hair walked out in front of the headlights. Frank and Joe both recognized him. It was Conrad Daye.

"I just want to talk," he called out.

"He's got a funny way of starting a conversation," Joe growled.

"Come on, Frank!" Daye shouted. "Just give me a couple of minutes. Hear me out, and then you can go."

Frank opened his door and started to climb out of the van.

Joe grabbed his brother's shoulder. "What are you doing?" he asked sharply. "It could be a trap!"

"It's a little late to worry about that," Frank said calmly. "We don't exactly have a lot of options right now."

Joe knew his brother was right. They could go out and face Conrad Daye, or they could wait for him—and maybe some of his friends—to come get them. "Okay," he said, letting go of Frank's shoulder. "But I'm going with you."

They both jumped out of the van and walked over to Conrad Daye. "Next time try the phone," Frank said. "It's a lot easier—and safer."

Daye shook his head. "I had to see you in person."

"You could have called and made an appointment," Joe snapped.

Daye snorted. "Yeah, right. Then you could have brought your cop buddies along. They're real eager to get their hands on me, thanks to you."

His eyes locked on Frank. "Why are you going to all this trouble to set me up? What did I ever do to you?"

"What are you talking about?" Frank replied. "What makes you think we're trying to set you up?"

"Because *somebody* is," Daye answered gruffly, "and you Boy Scouts keep popping up with all the pieces the cops need to build a nice little frame for me."

Frank returned Daye's glare with his own steady gaze. "It's a frame job only if you're not guilty."

"And if you're not guilty," Joe said, "you should turn yourself in and tell your side of the story."

Daye let out a bitter laugh. "What fairy tale did you fall out of? Get real. I'm no angel, and the cops would love an excuse to clip my wings. They're not going to ask a lot of questions if someone hands them my head on a platter."

"If you're not guilty," Frank replied, "how do you explain your fingerprints on the shoe box?"

Daye scowled. "What are you talking about? What shoe box? The warrant's for assault and attempted murder. Nobody cares if I boosted a pair of shoes."

"This box was full of plastic explosive," Frank told him.

"What?" Daye responded. He looked surprised. "Where would I get something like that? I wouldn't know the difference between plastic explosive and Play-Doh."

"I believe you," Frank said. He had been studying Daye carefully the whole time, and the gang leader seemed sincere. The clincher had been the question about the shoe box. Frank had deliberately left out any mention of the contents to see if Daye would slip up. But his shocked reaction couldn't have been better if it were rehearsed. If Daye did know about the plastic explosives, then he had a promising career as an actor.

Joe looked at his brother. He didn't know what Frank had in mind, but he figured he'd better play along. "Maybe we can help you," Joe said. "But you'll have to turn yourself in first."

Daye whirled and aimed a finger at Joe. "You don't want to help me. You only want to see me behind bars."

"No, you're wrong," Frank said evenly. "We only want to find the truth. And, believe me, we *will* find it."

"I hope so," Daye replied. "But don't expect me to roll over and play dead in the meantime."

He turned around and walked back to his car. "Don't try to follow me," he called back as he opened the door.

"We can still grab him," Joe whispered.

Frank shook his head. "What would you do in his place?"

Joe watched as Daye backed out of the dead end and drove away. "Probably bug out and lay low," he admitted.

Frank clapped his brother on the back. "What do you say we call it a night? There's nothing in that basement that won't still be there tomorrow."

"That's true," Joe replied. "There's also nothing in my stomach. If we hurry, we might get back home in time for dinner."

The next morning Joe woke up to the sun streaming in the window, remembered it was Saturday, and went back to sleep. He was just drifting off again when something shook the bed. He knew what it was. It could only be Frank, the human alarm clock.

Joe tried to ignore him. Maybe his brother would get bored and go away. But he didn't.

Frank leaned over the bed. "Are you still asleep?" he asked impatiently.

"No," Joe muttered. "I'm doing my homework. What does it look like?"

"It looks like I'll be going to the self-defense center by myself," Frank answered as he walked out of the room. "Unless you're downstairs and ready to hit the road in fifteen minutes."

Sixteen minutes later Joe bolted out the front door, clutching his jacket in one hand. He ran down the driveway, chasing the black van as it rolled out into the street. "Wait up!" he called out.

Frank stuck his head out the driver's side window. "You're late!" he yelled back. He shifted into first gear and started off down the street.

Joe hurled his jacket onto the pavement. "That's not fair!" he shouted. He stared at the back of the van as it moved away. He was about to go back into the house when the van stopped and the door swung open. He scooped up his jacket and sprinted across the lawn.

"Were you really going to take off and leave me standing in the driveway?" Joe asked as he climbed into the van. "Just because I was a minute late?"

"Time waits for no man," Frank replied.

Joe shot a look at him. "What's *that* supposed to mean?"

Frank shrugged. "Beats me. Sure sounds impressive, though—doesn't it?"

When they got to Madison Street Frank pulled into the parking lot of the Bayport Savings Bank.

"What are we doing here?" Joe asked as they got out of the van. "Opening a new account?"

"I just want to see how Chet's doing," Frank said. "It'll only take a minute."

The inside of the bank was a time warp, a relic from another era. Dark wood paneling and trim, ornate plaster molding where the walls met the ceiling. There was even a chandelier hanging in the middle of the large lobby.

Big, burly Chet Morton looked almost comical standing behind the bars of the old-fashioned teller's cage. Frank noticed that Chet still had a large bandage on his forehead, but apparently the wound wasn't serious enough to keep him away from work.

Since Chet wasn't waiting on a customer, the Hardys ambled right up to the counter. "What've they got you in for?" Joe asked with a grin.

"Very funny," Chet said in a low voice. His eyes darted around the bank. "If my boss sees you guys hanging around, I could get in big trouble."

"Relax," Frank said. "We just wanted to say hello and make sure you were doing okay."

"Yeah," Joe said. "We haven't seen you since we pulled you out of the gutter."

Chet's hand went up to the bandage on his forehead. "It took twelve stitches," he said. "The doctor thinks it might even leave a scar. Want to see?"

Frank grimaced. "Ah, not right now," he answered. "Maybe some other time."

Chet looked disappointed.

Frank turned around and saw Sam White pushing through the revolving door into the lobby. "Hey, Chet," he whispered, "do you know that guy?"

Chet looked up. "What guy? Oh, you mean Mr. White? According to my boss, he's one of the bank's best customers." Chet frowned slightly. "But I don't think I've ever actually seen him make a deposit with any of the tellers. He just heads straight downstairs."

"Downstairs?" Joe echoed. "What's downstairs?"

"Two vaults," Chet said. "One of them is a safe deposit vault. I don't know what Mr. White keeps down there, but he comes in two or three times a week."

"Come on," Joe said, nudging his brother. "Let's get over to the self-defense center. That's what you got me out of bed for, remember?"

Kay Lewis was out in front of the building when they drove up, but she didn't notice them. She was absorbed in a complex, flowing set of body movements that looked more like ballet than any fighting style Joe had ever seen.

"Hey, Kay!" he called out as he hopped out of the van. "Did you decide to give up martial arts for modern dance?"

She stopped in midmotion, one leg in the air and one arm extended skyward. She slowly turned her head in Joe's direction. Despite her awkward pose, Joe thought she looked relaxed. No, that wasn't the right word. Serene. Yes, she looked serene.

Kay shifted to a more normal pose and smiled. "These movements are called t'ai chi ch'uan," she said. "It's sort of a mental *and* physical workout. Or maybe meditation is a better word for it. But it's also a highly effective form of self-defense," she added. "Come here and I'll show you."

She stood facing Joe, legs apart, knees slightly bent, arms hanging loose at her sides. "In judo," Kay said, "you go with your opponent's force, using his own strength to throw him off balance or to flip him. T'ai chi is like that—except you channel your opponent's force through your body and right back at him."

"How do you do that?" Frank asked.

"Your brother's going to help me demonstrate," she replied. She turned her attention back to Joe. "I'm a wall. Try to move me."

"Huh?"

"Just try to push me back. Shove me or something."

Joe reached out and jabbed at her chest half-heartedly.

"Come on," she chided him. "You can do better than that."

Joe reached out and shoved hard on her left shoulder. It yielded easily as she swiveled from the waist. At the same time, her right arm swung out in a wide arc. The heel of her palm stopped a hairbreadth from Joe's left temple.

"See what I mean?" Kay said.

Joe nodded. "I think so."

She patted him on the back. "Maybe you should take my class. You might learn something. But I bet you didn't rush over here at this hour of the morning to sign up."

"We wanted to take a closer look at that room in the basement," Frank said.

"No problem," Kay replied. "Let's go."

Kay led the way down to the basement and stood by the steel door while Frank and Joe inspected the crumbling old potbellied stove. "Checking out its antique value?" she joked.

Frank tugged on the stovepipe that led into the brick wall. "Actually," he said, "I want to see what's on the other side of this wall. This pipe has to go somewhere."

He pulled on the smokestack again, but it was jammed in tight. "Do you have something I could use to pry this thing out?" he asked.

"Sorry," Kay replied. "I'm not into tools." She gestured to the wooden shelves on the wall. "Why don't you try one of those boards?"

"Good idea," Joe said. He ran his hands over the shelves, looking for a loose board that they could use as a lever. He found one that wasn't nailed down on one end. He was about to try to yank it off the wall when he saw something strange. The shelf was hinged at the other end.

"Hey, Frank," he said, lifting up the loose end of the shelf, "what do you make of this?"

Frank didn't know what to make of it. He was too stunned to say anything. Because when Joe lifted the shelf a crack opened in the wall, running from the floor to the ceiling.

Frank touched the crack, and a section of the wall swung open.

Chapter 9

FRANK PEERED INSIDE the opening. There was just enough light coming from behind him to reveal a few rotted wooden steps that led down to a dirt floor. Beyond that was blackness.

"The secret entrance to the hidden vault!" Joe cried.

Frank didn't say anything. Even if there was a vault, it was more likely to be filled with fat spiders than gold bars. Still, there was something down there, and Frank was just as eager as Joe to find out what it was.

Frank prodded the first stair with his foot. The wood felt soft and spongy. "I don't think this will hold our weight," he said.

Joe looked down at the dirt floor. It looked solid enough—and there were only three steps anyway. "No problem," he said with a grin. And before his brother could say anything Joe leapt out over the stairs and landed on the floor with a soft thud.

"Well, now that you're down there," Frank said, "can you see anything?"

Joe looked around. It was too dark to see any details, but at one end of the space he could make out a dim outline. "I think there's a door here," he said. "See if Kay has a flashlight."

Frank turned to ask her, but she was gone. A moment later she appeared in the doorway again, waving a flashlight. "I thought we might need this," she said. "I doubt if we'll find a light switch down there." She handed the flashlight to Frank. "Now let's see what we've got."

Frank thumbed the switch and then twisted the focus to widen the beam. Joe was standing in a narrow passageway. The walls were rock and earth, held back by wood struts. The ceiling was wood planks supported by sagging two-by-fours. Some of the planks had buckled and split apart, and loose piles of dirt had collected on the floor beneath them.

Frank aimed the light past Joe, and the beam glinted off a steel door set in a brick wall that appeared to bulge outward.

"When I bought this place," Kay remarked, "nobody told me it came with all this extra hardware." She looked down at Joe. "How is it down there?"

"Okay," Joe replied. "But a little too rustic for my taste."

"Well, stand back," Kay told him. "If I own it, I want to check it out for myself." She hopped over the stairs and landed nimbly next to Joe.

Joe motioned to Frank. "Toss me the flash and jump down."

"Hang on a sec," Frank responded. Sitting down on the edge of the opening, he bent down and pried loose the top step. Then he took the board and wedged it in the narrow gap where the secret door was hinged to the wall. "I don't know how to open this thing from the other side," he explained. "This way I won't have to worry about it."

Satisfied that the door couldn't shut by accident, Frank entered the subterranean tunnel.

Joe played the beam over the door at the other end of the passageway. It was the same design as the other two steel doors. This time Frank got the honor of cranking it open. But instead of a second door on the other side they were greeted with a cold, dank, musty odor.

It didn't smell really bad, Joe thought, just old. Shining the flashlight inside, he could see, about ten feet ahead, another brick wall.

Stepping inside, Joe slipped and almost fell on the mud-slick surface. Frank grabbed him, but Joe lost his grip on the flashlight. It tumbled to the ground and skittered a few feet down a slight incline. Beyond it the ground sloped up again until it joined with the wall on the other side.

Balancing carefully, Frank followed Joe in. He eased down to the bottom and picked up the flashlight. There were no walls to the right or left. They were in a long, dark tunnel. Frank looked at the mud- and slime-covered bricks. He could hear the steady sound of dripping water somewhere, but it was hard to tell if it was close by or far away.

"Looks like some kind of sewer," Kay Lewis observed as she slid down into the tunnel.

Frank shot a nervous glance back up at the door.

"Don't worry," Kay said. "I propped it open with a good-size rock."

Frank relaxed. "Good. It looks like this whole thing was meant to be strictly a one-way street."

"What about this?" Joe asked, gesturing to the tunnel around them. "You don't think Jake Barton built this, do you?"

Frank shook his head. "No. I think Kay is right. It's a sewer."

Joe stared down at his feet and grimaced. "You mean we're standing in . . ." His words trailed off.

"Relax," Frank said. "I don't think this sewer gets a lot of use anymore. They haven't made them out of brick for a long time. Bayport's an old city. This may be a section of the original sewer system—before they put in the deeper concrete sewers."

Kay Lewis looked around. "Well, with a little work this might make a swell bomb shelter—but why do you think a gangster like Barton would have been interested in the sewer system?"

Frank smiled. "That's easy. This was his emergency escape route."

"Escape to where?" Joe responded.

Frank pointed the flashlight down the dark tunnel. "Let's find out."

Frank led the way, picking out a path through the debris. It was hard to tell what lay ahead of them for more than a few feet. The beam from the light turned every rock and angle into a giant, jumpy shadow form.

It was slow going, but before long they came to a mound of rubble choking the tunnel.

"Looks like the end of the line," Joe said.

"So we backtrack and go the other way," Frank replied.

"I've got a better idea," Kay said. "Let's backtrack on out of here. I've had enough spelunking for one day—and I've got a class to teach soon."

"We can't quit now!" Joe protested.

"Relax," Frank said. "The tunnel's not going anywhere. We can come back tomorrow. Besides, the most exciting thing we're likely to find is an old manhole sealed up years ago."

Joe sighed. "You're probably right. Barton could have used the sewer to go just about anywhere in Bayport."

"I doubt if he ever went very far," Frank said with a grin. "Back then, people still used this sewer."

* * *

Joe squinted against the bright sun when they walked out the front door of the self-defense center. He had almost forgotten it was daytime. In fact, it wasn't even noon yet. It was almost as if time had stood still while they wandered through the lightless underworld.

Thinking about it, he also realized that his sense of direction had vanished underground. He had no idea if the sewer tunnel ran north–south or east–west or on some angle in between.

He stopped thinking when he saw Sam White strolling up to the building. "What are *you* doing here?" Joe demanded.

"Maybe I'm just taking a walk," the developer replied evenly. "Or maybe I'm here to have a talk with Ms. Lewis." He walked up the steps and faced Joe. "Either way, it's none of your business."

Joe scowled. "And what, exactly, is *your* business? Supplying street gangs with the latest high-tech firepower?"

White turned to Frank. "What is he talking about?"

Frank answered with a question. "You do a lot of blasting in your work, right?"

"Depends on what you mean by a lot," White replied.

"I'll take that as a yes," Frank said. "And you have a permit to use plastic explosive, right?"

"Sure," the developer responded. "For some

jobs it's the best thing. It gives you a controlled blast. So what?"

Frank looked straight at him. "So somebody blew up Kay Lewis's car—and then we found enough plastic explosive to put this building into orbit."

"And you think I did it?" White asked sharply. "Stop reading comic books and grow up. There are lots of powerful, successful people who also happen to be honest. I don't threaten people, and I don't put bombs in their cars. I came by here to tell Kay that my offer's good for forty-eight more hours. After that I'll go ahead and build the shopping center even without this piece of property.

"And if I wanted to blow up this old pile of bricks," he added as he walked away, "there wouldn't be enough left for you to fill a shoe box." Then he whirled around, stomped back down the steps, and stormed off down the street.

Frank and Joe exchanged a glance. "Who said anything about a shoe box?" Frank said.

"Maybe it's just a coincidence," Joe suggested.

"I don't believe in coincidences," Frank replied.

Kay Lewis poked her head out the door. "What are you guys doing hanging around? I figured you'd be gone by now, but I told him I'd check anyway."

"Told who?" Frank asked.

"The guy on the phone," Kay answered. "He wants to talk to you, Frank."

Frank looked at his brother. "Who knows we're here?"

"There's one easy way to find out," Joe replied, nodding toward the door.

Frank went inside and picked up the phone. "Hello," he said. "Who is this?"

"Bayport's most wanted," came the reply.

Frank recognized the voice. It was Conrad Daye. "How'd you know where to find us?" Frank asked.

"The same way I know where your girlfriend lives," Daye said icily. "I had you tailed."

A chill ran down Frank's spine. "What do you mean? You haven't done anything to Callie, have you?"

"Not yet," Daye answered. The threat was crystal clear in his tone. "But all sorts of things *could* happen to her—depending on what you do in the next few minutes."

Frank clutched the phone so tightly his knuckles turned white. "What do you want?" he asked in a strained voice.

There was a nervous chuckle on the other end of the line. "What do I want?" Conrad Daye echoed. "I want a Ferrari convertible with snakeskin seats. No, wait. I want a happy home and a college scholarship. How's that, Frank? I want to be just like you."

"Listen," Frank said, struggling to sound calm, "I know that—"

"No!" Daye snapped, cutting him off. "You listen. Be at eight-twelve Lincoln in ten minutes. Got that?"

"I'll be there," Frank replied.

"And come alone," Daye added, "or I cut the girl."

Chapter 10

THE LINE WENT DEAD. Frank slammed the phone down.

"What was that all about?" Kay Lewis asked him.

Frank took a deep breath. "Daye's got Callie."

"We should've taken down that punk last night," Joe said bitterly. "What does he want? Some kind of ransom?"

Frank glanced at his watch. "He wants to meet me in nine minutes."

"Then we better get going," Joe replied.

Frank shook his head. "He told me not to bring anybody else."

"Then we'll be your backup," Joe said. "We'll follow you in another car."

"It's too risky," Frank argued. "And there's no time to find a car." He looked at his brother. "I'm sorry, Joe. I've got to do this alone." Then he bolted out the front door and ran to the van.

"He's going to need some insurance," Kay said.

Joe nodded. "I know—but what can we do?"

Kay smiled. "I've got great insurance—and a brand-new car to prove it. Want to take it out for a spin?"

Frank screeched the van to a halt at a stoplight. He checked the time. It was about thirty seconds later than the last time he had checked. He still had four minutes. That should be enough time, he told himself, but it would be tight. He looked around. The intersection was clear. There were no other cars in sight. Frank gritted his teeth and punched the accelerator, leaving the red light behind.

He got to the address on Lincoln with about a minute to spare. The building was a burnt-out skeleton. Frank could see the sky through the windows on the upper floor. Half the roof was missing. He double-checked the number, 812. That's what Daye had said. He was sure of it.

Then Frank spotted a car up the street. He could see two people sitting in it, but it was too far away for Frank to make out any details. He started to walk toward the car when he heard a phone ring behind him.

A phone? Frank spun around and saw a pay phone on the sidewalk about fifty feet away. He hadn't noticed it before because it was partially blocked by a utility pole. He sprinted over and grabbed the receiver, almost ripping the metal-sheathed cord out of the phone base.

"What kind of game is this?" he shouted into the phone.

"One where I make the rules," Conrad Daye's voice said in Frank's ear. "Don't forget that."

"I won't," Frank said grimly. "What do you want me to do now?"

"Be at the video arcade in five minutes," Daye told him. "And don't hang up the phone. Leave it off the hook."

Frank dropped the receiver and left it dangling there. He ran back to the van and took off again. Daye wasn't taking any chances, he realized. Frank could make it to the arcade in five minutes—if he didn't make any detours or stops along the way. And the bit with the phone was to prevent him from making any quick calls to tell anyone where he was going. Daye wouldn't hang up on his end until Frank was moving again.

The car Frank had spotted before was probably his "escort," making sure he stuck to the game plan. His eyes darted to the side mirror. There it was, keeping back far enough to avoid attracting Frank's attention but dogging his every move, as though he were dragging it behind him on an invisible leash.

Frank pulled up in front of the storefront arcade right on time. Dave Gilson was waiting for him at the door.

"Follow me," Gilson ordered.

Inside there were about a half dozen Scorpions. Gilson led Frank to a back room where another gang member stood by a door with a red Exit sign above it. Suddenly Gilson grabbed the collar of Frank's jacket and shoved him up against the wall. "Assume the position," he snarled.

Frank leaned forward, putting his weight on his arms, his palms flat against the wall.

Gilson patted him down. "Okay," he said. "Let's go."

The other gang member pushed open the door, and Gilson prodded Frank out into the alley behind the building. Frank wasn't surprised to see a car there.

"Get in," Gilson said gruffly as he walked around to the driver's side.

Frank studied Gilson intently as they drove in silence. Some guys joined gangs because it was the easiest way to survive in a rough neighborhood. But Frank had a feeling Dave Gilson got off on the violence. He liked pushing people around. If it wasn't for the Scorpions, he'd just be another school-yard bully—the kind Conrad Daye used to go after with a baseball bat.

A few minutes later Gilson pulled into the driveway of a ramshackle bungalow. Like too many houses in this part of town, it had a weather-beaten For Sale sign on the front lawn. Frank didn't think the owners had waited for a buyer before they picked up and moved on.

Gilson hammered on the front door. "It's me, Rad," he said loudly. "Open up."

"Why don't you just get a bullhorn and make a public announcement?" Frank suggested.

Gilson glared at him. "Watch your mouth or I'll—"

"Yeah, yeah," Frank cut him off. "I know. You'll cut my tongue out. Don't you know any other threats?"

Gilson moved toward Frank and lashed out with his right hand.

That was exactly what Frank wanted him to do. He easily sidestepped the blow. He grabbed Gilson's wrist with his right hand, yanking it forward and twisting it at the same time. Then he brought his left forearm down sharply on Gilson's exposed elbow.

Gilson cried out in pain and clutched at his injured arm.

"Chill out and back off!" someone shouted.

Frank whirled around. Callie was standing in the doorway. Conrad Daye was behind her, his arm around her neck, a knife pressed against her throat.

Joe and Kay sat in the car, keeping an eye on the entrance to the video arcade.

"I think Frank spotted us back at the pay phone," Joe said.

"Does it matter?" Kay asked.

Joe shrugged. "I guess not."

"He should be glad he has a backup," Kay pointed out.

Joe chuckled. "You don't know Frank Hardy. Everything has to go according to plan—*his* plan." He glanced at the clock on the dashboard. "How long has he been in there, anyway?"

"About fifteen minutes," Kay replied.

"I don't like this," Joe muttered. "It doesn't add up. This is the last place Daye would show his face right now."

"Sometimes," Kay said, "the best place to hide is in plain sight."

Joe shook his head. "I don't think Daye is in there—and I don't think Frank is, either."

"You think we've been suckered?" Kay asked.

Joe opened the door and got out of the car. "That's what I'm about to find out."

Kay got out, too. "You know," she said as they walked toward the arcade, "I teach my students to avoid this kind of situation."

"Yeah—but I'm not one of your students," Joe reminded her.

"Too bad. You might learn something."

"That's what everybody keeps telling me."

Nobody was guarding the door this time. A few heads turned when Joe and Kay walked in, but they quickly turned away again.

Joe scanned the dimly lit room. There was no sign of Conrad Daye or Frank. Joe moved toward the back of the game room. Kay followed close behind. When they neared the door to the back room one of the gang members drifted out of the shadows and blocked the door.

Joe glanced over his shoulder. Three more Scorpions had closed in from behind.

"We don't want any trouble," the one blocking the door said.

"Too bad," Joe replied. "You should have thought of that before you grabbed my brother."

"We don't know what you're talking about," someone said.

"Just walk away and nobody gets hurt," another voice added.

"Tell me where my brother is," Joe said, "and we'll leave."

"And if we don't?"

Joe's lips curled back in a grim smile. "Then I'll be in your face and all over the place."

One of the gang members let out a harsh laugh. "Let's get it on," he rasped.

Kay Lewis tugged on Joe's arm. "Let's get out of here," she said nervously.

"What?" Joe responded in surprise.

"I really think we should leave," Kay urged him. *"Please."* It was almost a whine.

Joe couldn't believe it. Kay had suddenly turned into a—well, a *girl*. "Terrific," he muttered. "Sorry, guys," he said sourly. "It was all a big mistake. Never mind. Just forget the whole thing."

Joe and Kay started to walk back toward the front door. The Scorpions parted to let them by.

Kay brushed past one of them on the left—and whipped her right leg up and back in a blurring motion, hitting him just below and behind the knee. As he staggered backward her right arm shot across his chest. Gripping his right shoulder and using her extended leg as a fulcrum, she flung him to the floor.

Before anybody could even blink she was on top of him, pinning one arm with her knee. Her right fist hovered over his throat, a coiled snake poised to strike.

"Tell us where Frank Hardy is right now," she said calmly, "or I'll crush your windpipe. You'll die screaming—but nobody will hear you."

Frank slowly backed away from Dave Gilson, keeping his eyes locked on the knife at Callie's throat. "Let's *all* chill out," he said to Conrad Daye. "Your pal took a swing at me, so I returned the favor. That's all."

"You okay?" Daye asked Gilson.

Gilson rubbed his arm. "Yeah. He's all yours now. You want me to stick around?"

Daye shook his head. "I can handle it."

Gilson shot a silent parting glare at Frank and then walked back to the car.

"Get inside," Daye ordered. He backed up, pulling Callie with him.

Frank followed them into the house and closed the door. "Are you all right?" he asked Callie.

She tried to smile. "I've been better."

"You've got me now," Frank said to Daye. "How about letting her go?"

"Not until we get a few things cleared up," Daye replied.

"I'm listening," Frank said.

"You've got to convince the cops that I wasn't involved in any of those attacks."

"I need proof."

"Then get some," Daye snapped, his grip tightening on the knife.

"Okay," Frank said quickly. "Okay. Just don't—"

"Conrad Daye!" a voice blared through a bullhorn outside. "We have a warrant for your arrest! Release the hostages and come out with your hands up!"

Daye glared at Frank. He pressed the knife blade against Callie's throat. "I told you I'd cut her if you brought the cops," he snarled. "And I always keep my word."

Chapter 11

FRANK LUNGED FORWARD, reaching desperately for the knife.

"No!" Callie shouted. She grabbed Daye's arm with both hands, slamming her right foot down on his instep at the same time. Then she twisted toward him, bending at the waist, and backed out of the choke hold.

Still gripping Daye's arm with both hands, she stepped around him, jerking his arm up behind his back. She followed that with a rapid side kick into the back of his knee.

Daye staggered, but he didn't go down—and he still clutched the knife in his hand. He broke free of Callie's grip and spun around to face Frank. "Come on, Frank," he growled. "Let's finish it."

Frank took a slight step to the left, and Daye thrust at him with an underhand jab. But Frank's move was only a feint. He leapt to the outside of Daye's knife hand on the right. He grabbed Daye's wrist with one hand and his upper arm with the other. Then Frank side-kicked him in the back of the knee, aiming for the same spot Callie had hit.

Daye's knee buckled. Frank brought the knife arm down, pulling sharply with both hands, and smashed it against his leg. Daye's hand jerked open. The knife popped out and skittered across the floor.

Daye dove after it, but Callie was there first. She scooped it up and hurled it toward the window. The glass shattered, and the knife was gone.

The front door burst open. "Freeze!" a commanding voice barked.

"Don't shoot!" Frank yelled. He stepped between Conrad Daye and the muzzles of a half dozen automatic rifles and service revolvers. "Everything's under control," Frank said slowly and calmly.

The police moved into the room quickly. One of them holstered his weapon and handcuffed Daye's hands behind his back.

The gang leader looked at Frank. "You almost got your girlfriend killed. Is locking me up that important to you?"

Frank shook his head. "I didn't call the police. I didn't even know where I was going—and you made sure nobody could follow me with that switch back at video arcade. So you tell me how I managed to lead half the Bayport police force right to your hideout."

"*Somebody* told them," Daye insisted.

"Who knew you were here?" Callie asked Daye.

"Nobody," he replied. He paused for a second. "Nobody except Dave Gilson."

"Could you really have killed that guy with just one blow?" Joe asked Kay as they walked out of the gang hangout.

"I don't know," Kay said honestly. "I've never tried. But I think *he* believed I could—and that's all that really matters, isn't it?"

Joe nodded. "So he was probably telling the truth about Gilson being the only one who knows where Daye is holed up."

"The only way to find out is to find Dave Gilson," Kaye replied. "Any ideas on where to start looking?"

A patrol car pulled up next to them. "Uh-oh," Joe whispered. "Better let me handle this." He strolled up to the driver's window and smiled. "Is there some kind of problem, officer?"

The back door of the car opened. "No problem," Frank said with a grin as he got out.

"Nothing we couldn't handle ourselves," Callie chimed in, joining Frank on the sidewalk.

"Frank!" Joe called out. "Callie! Are you guys okay?" The words rushed out in a torrent. "What happened? Where were you? Where's Daye? What are you doing here?"

"Whoa!" Frank said. "One question at a time.

We'll start with the last one. We came to pick up the van."

He glanced over Joe's shoulder at the video arcade. A couple of the Scorpions were watching them from the doorway. "I'll tell you the rest later," he said. "First, let's get out of here."

When the sun peeked over the horizon the next morning the first rays slanted down on the black van, bounced off the side mirror, and drilled right through Joe's eyelids. He rubbed his eyes and sat up slowly. "What time is it?" he yawned.

"Six-fifteen," Frank told him.

"I don't know why we had to come down here so early," Joe said, squinting out at a shabby ranch house. "Guys like Gilson never roll out of the sack before noon."

"Maybe I should have gotten a copy of his schedule from his secretary," Frank replied. "But that would have spoiled all the fun of getting up at five in the morning to sit in a cold van, drinking cold coffee."

"Okay," Joe said. "You made your point. But we could be sitting out here for hours while he's in there snoring away."

Frank sighed. "It's a stakeout, Joe. That's what it's all about—sitting around and waiting."

"Hold on," Joe said, leaning forward to get a better view. "Maybe I spoke too soon."

Frank looked out the windshield. The front door of the house had opened, and Dave Gilson walked out into the early morning light. He closed and locked the door and then headed for his car. Frank had spotted the car earlier—it was the one he had taken a ride in the day before.

He watched Gilson get in the car and waited for the rumble of its engine before starting up the van. Gilson drove off. Frank checked the side mirror. Another car was coming down the street. Good, Frank thought. He let the car pass and then pulled in behind it.

Since the cab of the van was higher than most cars, Frank could let several cars get between them and still keep track of Gilson. It was a trick he used often. Even when a suspect was on the lookout for a tail, he usually didn't look beyond the first couple of cars. So Frank just dropped back and relaxed.

They followed Gilson to a small park and watched from the van as he got out of his car and strolled over to a bench on the grass. There was a man sitting on the bench. Frank and Joe both recognized him.

"Okay," Joe said. "What's the connection between Dave Gilson and Patrick Smith?"

"Good question," Frank replied. "Too bad I don't have the answer."

The realtor and the gang member talked for a few minutes, and Smith handed something to Gilson. It was too small and too far away for the Hardys to tell what it was. Then the older man got up and walked off, and Gilson went back to his car.

Frank opened his door and slid out of the van.

"Where are you going?" Joe asked.

"I'm going to follow Smith," Frank told him. "You stick with Gilson."

"I'm glue," Joe said, moving over to the driver's seat. He gave Gilson a good head start before he put the van in gear and took off after him.

Bayport was starting to wake up, and there was more traffic now. That was fine with Joe. It meant there was less chance that Gilson would spot him.

Joe wasn't too surprised when Gilson turned down Madison—it was one way to get to the Scorpions' hangout. But Gilson wasn't headed for the video arcade. He stopped just up the street from the self-defense center.

Joe made an abrupt turn down a side street so Gilson wouldn't see him. He did a quick and dirty parking job and jumped out of the van. Peering around the corner, he saw Gilson walk up to the front door of Kay Lewis's building.

Gilson looked around furtively and then pulled something out of his pocket. Joe realized it was a key. He watched Gilson unlock the door and slip inside.

Joe jogged across the street and approached the building cautiously. Kay's new car wasn't anywhere in sight. That meant she probably wasn't in the building. Joe breathed a little easier.

He went up the steps and tried the door. It was open. He stuck his head inside and listened carefully. There were muffled sounds coming from the basement. What was Gilson doing down there?

Joe tiptoed to the stairwell. He cocked his head to one side and strained to hear any noise coming from below. Now there was nothing. He waited a few minutes, but waiting wasn't his strong suit. He decided to check it out.

He crept down the stairs quietly. There was no sign of Gilson in the main part of the basement. Joe could see that the double steel doors were wide open. But Gilson wasn't in the small room, either.

Then Joe noticed that the concealed entrance to the underground passage wasn't closed all the way. But before he could take a closer look he heard a hollow creaking sound, like rusty hinges in an echo chamber. The steel door leading to the old sewer! A few seconds later the brick wall started to swing open.

Joe darted back into the basement and crouched behind the furnace just seconds before Gilson came through the double doors and headed up the stairs. Joe waited until he heard the front door shut before coming out of his hiding place.

So Gilson knew about the secret way into the old sewer. But what was he doing down there? Joe had to find out.

Joe went through the back-to-back steel doors and grabbed the flashlight that Kay Lewis had left on the bookshelf. Then he lifted the hinged shelf that opened the secret door in the brick wall and went down the narrow corridor to the abandoned sewer.

Some distance down the sewer tunnel Joe saw an eerie glow that seemed to come out of the wall of the sewer. Joe switched off the flash beam and crept toward the dim light. As he got closer he could see that it was coming from a low side passage. If not for the light filtering through the opening, Joe would have missed it—as he and the others had before—even with his flashlight on.

Joe had to duck slightly to get past the mouth of the passage. But there was a little more headroom on the other side. Ahead he could see the familiar shape of a steel door with a lever-style handle. Jake Barton must have gotten a quantity discount at a closeout sale, Joe thought. The door was half open, and the glow was coming from the other side of the door.

Joe heard a noise and froze in his tracks. He cocked his head and listened. All he could pick up was the faint dripping of water somewhere—and the pounding of his own heart in his chest. He moved closer to the door.

Well, you've come this far, he told himself. You sure aren't going back without finding out what's in there. Joe took a deep breath and went through the doorway.

He found himself in a brick-lined chamber about the same size as the one connected to Kay's basement. The source of the light was a kerosene lantern on the floor.

Joe heard a creaking sound behind him. He whirled around just in time to see the metal door slam shut with a loud clank.

Just like the other steel doors, this one had a handle on only one side—and Joe was on the wrong side. He was trapped!

Chapter 12

IT WAS TURNING OUT to be a day of surprises.

Frank followed Patrick Smith to a fancy restaurant a few blocks from the park. Smith met a woman at the entrance, and they went in together.

The woman was Kay Lewis.

Frank was bewildered. First the early-morning meeting with that punk Gilson, and now this. What was Smith up to? And how was Kay mixed up in it?

If Joe had been there, he probably would have argued for what he liked to call an "ambush interview." His theory was that if you caught people by surprise, you were more likely to get the truth out of them. Sometimes it worked, and sometimes it backfired with a vengeance—leaving Frank to clean up the mess.

Frank decided to wait across the street from the restaurant. Kay and the realtor sat in a booth by the window. Frank pretended to be interested in the latest women's shoe styles in a storefront display window while keeping an eye on the unlikely couple reflected in the glass.

After two hours Frank wasn't any closer to unraveling the mystery of the meeting in the restaurant—but he was pretty sure he had deciphered the key to success in the high-heel market.

Finally Kay Lewis and Patrick Smith got up and left the restaurant. They paused on the sidewalk outside, shook hands, and walked off in opposite directions.

Frank decided to stick with the realtor. Smith's office was nearby, and Frank surmised that was exactly where Smith was headed.

Frank had a few questions he wanted to ask Smith, but he didn't think he'd be able to pry loose any useful information if he confronted the slick salesman on his home turf. So he decided to rip a page out of Joe Hardy's crime-stopper's textbook.

He jogged across the street and caught up with the real estate agent. "Mr. Smith!" he exclaimed in a surprised voice. "What a coincidence! I was just on my way to your office to see you."

"Well, that certainly *is* a coincidence," Smith agreed, flashing a toothy smile, "because I was just thinking about *you.*"

"Oh?" Frank replied. This was going to be tricky, he warned himself. Smith was a slippery one. He had meant to catch the realtor with his guard down, but instead it was Frank who was at a loss for words.

"Yes," Smith said. "An associate of mine tells me you're not convinced Conrad Daye was responsible for all those incidents around the self-defense school."

"Is that what Kay Lewis told you over breakfast?" Frank asked in a casual tone.

The realtor's smile faded. "If you're spying on me, you're wasting your time. I don't have anything to hide. My meeting with Ms. Lewis was legitimate business."

"And what about Dave Gilson?" Frank countered. "He doesn't look like the type who wants to invest in real estate."

Smith took a long look at Frank. "David Gilson is a troubled young man," he said in a somber tone. "He's also my nephew—my sister's son.

"This is really none of your business," he continued after a short pause. "But I have a feeling you're going to be a serious nuisance until you get some kind of answer.

"Dave's father died about five years ago, and the family's had a hard time making ends meet since then. I help out whenever I can. My sister's too proud to take the money herself, so I give it to Dave. I know he blows some of it, but most of it goes to pay the rent and buy food."

"I'm sorry," Frank said. "I didn't know."

"Of course you didn't," Smith replied curtly. "As I said, it's really none of your business. And if you have any more questions about my personal life, you can take them to the police."

He turned and walked away, leaving Frank standing on the sidewalk.

Frank made a mental note not to try that approach again—and underlined it. Now the surveillance was blown, and if Smith was up to anything shady, he would take extra care to cover his tracks from now on.

By the time Frank got home it was well past noon. There was no sign of the van, which meant Joe was still out. Either that or he had come home and then left again.

Frank headed for the kitchen to grab something to eat and ran into his aunt, Gertrude Hardy. She was sitting at the kitchen table, knitting something. Frank had no idea what it would eventually turn out to be. Right now it looked like a sweater for a boa constrictor.

Frank couldn't remember a time when his aunt hadn't been around. She was a permanent fixture in the Hardy household.

"You boys ran off again this morning without having breakfast," she scolded him.

"The fish won't wait while you sit around eating omelets," Frank said.

"The two of you must be the worst fishermen in Bayport," she remarked.

"What do you mean?" Frank asked.

"I mean you go on these early-morning fishing trips, but you never bring home any fish!"

Frank slapped his forehead. "You mean you're

supposed to keep them? Wait'll I tell Joe. All this time we've been throwing them back!"

"Speaking of your brother, where is he? Did you lose him in the bay?"

"He, ah, had some errands to run," Frank answered vaguely. "Has he called in or anything like that?"

Gertrude shook her head. "The phone hasn't rung once all day."

"Are you sure?" Frank asked her.

She peered at him over the top of her bifocals. "Is your brother in some kind of trouble?"

"I hope not," Frank muttered under his breath.

He went upstairs to his room and checked the telephone answering machine. There weren't any messages.

Frank had an uneasy feeling. He hadn't actually told Joe to check in at any specific time. It was just sort of a standard operating procedure. If they had to split up, they kept in touch by calling the house every few hours. If they were both out, they simply left messages on the machine. They could also listen to messages by punching in a replay code from any push-button phone.

Frank glanced at his watch. It was almost five hours since he had left Joe at the park. That wasn't too bad. If Gilson was on the move a lot, then Joe might not have had time to get to a phone. After all, Frank himself hadn't bothered to call in while he was tailing Patrick Smith.

He decided to give Joe a few more hours before hitting the panic button. In the meantime he had some research to do.

Shuffling through the papers next to his computer, Frank pulled out a brochure on the AAA Self-defense Center. Callie had given it to him when she was first thinking about signing up for the class. He scanned it quickly, refreshing his memory. If what it said was true, then Kay Lewis had spent a hefty chunk of her life absorbed in the martial arts: karate, kung-fu, aikido, judo, tae kwon do. She had studied weaponless combat all over the world.

So what was she doing in Bayport? This case kept turning up more questions than answers.

The phone rang once, and Frank snatched the receiver. "Hello?" he said expectantly.

"Boy, that was fast," a female voice said. "You must have been sitting on top of the phone. It barely had a chance to ring."

"Oh, hi, Callie," Frank said. He had hoped to hear Joe's voice on the other end.

"Is it my imagination," Callie said, "or are you less than thrilled that I called?"

"I'm sorry," Frank replied. "I was sort of expecting a call from Joe."

"Is anything wrong?" Callie asked.

"I don't know," Frank said. "I haven't seen him or heard from him since early this morning." He told her everything that had happened since he had last seen her, including the discovery of the abandoned sewer.

"Maybe we should go look for him," Callie suggested.

"I don't suppose you'd consider just lending me your car," Frank ventured.

"You know me so well," she replied. "You're right. I wouldn't. I'll pick you up in ten minutes."

After Joe made two or three complete checks of the sealed chamber he settled down for an intensely boring wait. The only contents of the vault were a pick and shovel, and as far as he could tell, they hadn't been used for anything yet. He debated hacking his way through the brick wall, but he figured the only thing he'd find on the other side would be another wall—a natural one made of rocks and dirt.

Sooner or later someone would get him out. It was a fairly safe bet that Gilson had locked him in. He had probably gone back to his car to get something he had forgotten—and when he returned and found Joe in the vault, he panicked and locked him in. Once Gilson figured out what to do he'd be back. Joe glanced at the pick. He planned to be ready.

Since there wasn't much he could do in the meantime, Joe decided to shut off the lantern and get some sleep.

Sometime later he woke with a start. He had no idea where he was or how much time had passed. When he finally remembered that he was in the vault he fumbled in his pocket for a match and lit the kerosene lantern. Maybe it was a waste of fuel, but Joe wasn't sleepy anymore, and he didn't feel like sitting around in the dark.

The lantern burned brightly for about an hour. Then it dimmed and sputtered out.

Joe switched on the flashlight and inspected the lantern. He couldn't see anything wrong with it. He picked it up and shook it lightly. There was still plenty of kerosene sloshing around in the base tank.

Joe sat down. It was hard to think. His chest heaved up and down as if he had just run a mile. He couldn't seem to get enough air.

That was it, he realized with dawning horror. The vault was running out of air!

Chapter 13

"SO WHERE DO WE START?" Callie asked Frank as they drove away from the house.

"Well," Frank said thoughtfully, "if we find Dave Gilson, Joe shouldn't be too far away."

"And if he isn't?" Callie asked.

"Then we find out what Gilson knows about it," Frank said grimly.

"So where do we find Gilson?"

"Let's try the Scorpions' hangout first."

While Callie drove, Frank replayed his conversation with Patrick Smith in his head. Except this time Frank was ready with all the right questions. Why did Smith meet Gilson in a deserted park instead of at his office? How did he know what Gilson did with the money? Didn't he feel a little uneasy handing over wads of cash to a member of a street gang? Wasn't there a more reliable way to help out his sister?

The mental image of Smith didn't answer. It just flashed a Cheshire-cat grin and slowly faded away until there was nothing left but shiny white teeth.

Frank gazed out the window. He didn't pay much attention to where they were until he caught a glimpse of a familiar shape on a side street, parked at a crazy angle. "Stop the car!" he shouted.

Callie hit the brakes, and the car squealed to a stop in the middle of the street. "What is it?" she asked in a startled voice.

But Frank was already out of the car, running toward the black van. The self-defense center was only a block away, he realized. It wasn't exactly the quickest way to the video arcade. Callie had simply taken the route that was familiar to her. Not that Frank was complaining.

He opened the door and looked inside the van. Everything seemed to be okay. The door was unlocked, and the parking job wasn't going to win any neatness awards. That meant Joe had been in a hurry. The engine block was cold. That meant the van had been sitting there for a while.

And all of that meant that Joe had still been hot on Gilson's trail when he left the van. So where did they go?

There was only one logical answer: the AAA Self-defense Center.

"Let's go see if Kay Lewis is home," Frank said to Callie. She had already parked her car.

"Do you think she knows anything about this?" Callie asked.

"It wouldn't hurt to ask," Frank responded.

Frank knocked loudly on the door several times

before Kay answered. She was wearing baggy sweat pants and a loose-fitting T-shirt.

"Oh, hi, guys," she said, wiping a trickle of sweat off her forehead. "I was just working out. Come on in."

Frank came right to the point. "Joe's missing. Have you seen him at all today?"

Kay shook her head. "No, I haven't seen him since you guys left here yesterday."

"The van's parked right down the street," Frank said. "Are you sure Joe didn't come by here?"

Kay eyed Frank with suspicion. "I didn't say that. I said I haven't seen him. There's a difference."

"I don't understand," Callie said. "What do you mean?"

"I mean I wasn't here most of the morning," Kay responded. There was an edge of impatience in her voice. "If he came around then, I wouldn't know about it."

"And where were you this morning?" Frank prodded, even though he already knew the answer.

"There was some kind of glitch in the paperwork when I bought this place. Patrick Smith had a stack of forms for me to sign, and he insisted on meeting at an overpriced restaurant that serves undercooked eggs."

Something clicked in Frank's mind. A few of the puzzle pieces fell into place. "Maybe Smith wanted to make sure you were anywhere but here during a certain time period,'' he said.

''Why would he want to do that?'' Kay asked.

''So somebody working for him could get in without being noticed.''

''But why?'' Kay persisted. ''I don't have anything worth stealing.''

''I don't know why,'' Frank admitted. ''Not yet, anyway. But I bet I know where the person went once he got in.''

''I bet I do, too,'' Callie said. ''Something tells me we're not the only ones who know about the old sewer line.''

''You don't think someone's down there now, do you?'' Kay asked doubtfully.

''All I know,'' Frank replied, ''is that there might be something down there that will help us find Joe. And that's all I care about right now.''

Without saying anything else he headed for the basement stairs. Kay glanced at Callie. Callie shrugged. Then they both followed Frank down to the underground chamber.

''Where's that flashlight of yours?'' Frank asked Kay.

She looked around the small room and frowned. ''I thought we left it over there.''

Frank followed her gaze to the shelf on the wall. ''Well, it isn't there now,'' he observed.

''I think I've got another one upstairs,'' Kay said.

While she went to get the flashlight Frank

took a close look at the wall, running his hand over the spot where he knew the concealed door would open. The only telltale sign was a hairline crack in the mortar, zigzagging between the bricks.

"Pretty slick work," he said. "You can't even see it from a couple of feet away."

"If you didn't already know where it was," Callie said, "you'd never find it."

Kay returned with the flashlight. "We're in business," she announced, thumbing the switch and shining the wide beam on the wall. "Let's hit it."

Since the hidden doorway in the brick wall was shut tight, Frank had to lift the hinged shelf to unlock it. The steel door at the end of the short passage was closed and latched, too.

"If anybody's in there now," Frank said as he pushed down on the handle, "they didn't plan to get out again. You can open these doors only from one side."

Inside the damp, dark sewer everything looked pretty much the same as it had the day before. Frank had no idea what he was looking for—maybe a big sign that flashed "Clue" in garish neon colors.

"Now what?" Callie prodded him, bringing Frank back to the bleak reality of the tunnel.

Frank shivered. Suddenly he felt very cold. And he had a bad feeling that if he didn't find Joe soon, it would be too late.

Somewhere, a faint clank echoed down the abandoned sewer. Frank stood still and listened.

Clank. There it was again, a hollow metallic sound.

"What's that noise?" Callie asked.

"Shhh!" Frank hissed, putting a finger to his lips.

Clank. Where was it coming from? It was hard to tell. The sound bounced off the crumbling walls. Frank moved a few steps in one direction.

Clank. No, it was coming from the other way. But it was fainter now.

"Give me the flashlight," he said urgently.

Frank moved down the tunnel slowly, waving the beam back and forth along the sewer walls. He couldn't hear the sound anymore. He stopped and listened.

Clank. There it was, just ahead and off to the left.

Frank trained the light on the curved wall and zeroed in on a low, narrow gap in the brick. The sound had to be coming from the other side of the wall. Crouching in the opening, he aimed the beam inside. The shaft of light stabbed through the darkness—and glinted off the steel door at the end of the short passage.

The sound had stopped completely now. The grisly meaning of the heavy silence struck Frank like a hammer blow. He plunged headlong into the corridor, grabbed the metal handle, and flung the door open.

Joe was lying facedown in the dirt, the pick handle clutched in his hand. Frank figured Joe had been trying to whack his way out. Frank rushed in and almost tripped over the kerosene lantern. He frantically kicked it out of the way and dragged his brother out of the vault.

Frank laid Joe down on his back, pried apart his lips, and forced air into his lungs with mouth-to-mouth breathing.

Kay Lewis rushed over. Dropping to her knees, she deftly placed one hand over the other on Joe's chest and started pumping with a steady rhythm. "One . . . two . . . three . . . four . . . five . . ." she counted as she pressed down firmly. Then she went back to one and started over. She kept repeating the five count in a calm, clear voice.

Every time she reached five Frank blew more air down Joe's throat. "Come on, Joe—breathe!" he whispered desperately.

". . . three . . . four . . ." Kay counted out.

A low rasping noise escaped from Joe's lips. Then suddenly his body was wracked by a violent burst of coughing. But at least he was breathing.

Frank leaned back against the wall with a heavy sigh. He was drained, but he still managed a weak smile for Kay Lewis. "Thanks," he said simply. He couldn't think of any other words to offer.

Joe struggled to a sitting position, blinking his eyes and looking around. "Hey, guys," he croaked. He cleared his throat and tried again. "Well," he said in a hoarse voice, "I'm never staying in *that* motel again. The rooms are filthy, and the service is lousy."

Frank got up, reached out, and helped Joe to his feet. "That kerosene lantern almost killed you," he said, nodding toward the vault. "It sucked up all the oxygen and spewed out carbon monoxide—kind of like sitting in a car with the engine running in a closed garage. Not a really smart thing to do."

"Thank you, Mr. Wizard," Joe grumbled. "I don't know what I'd do without your cheerful reports."

"You'd do what you always do. You never listen to me anyway." Frank took Joe's arm and draped it over his shoulder. "Come on—let's get out of here."

Kay took Joe's other arm, and Callie walked ahead with the flashlight.

Back in the main sewer tunnel it was easy to find the way back out. Light from the basement spilled through the open doorway in the wall.

"That's funny," Joe said thickly. He was still a little groggy. "It looks like the light's moving."

Frank could see that his brother was right. Long shadows flickered in the opening. Then a dark shape appeared in the doorway, outlined in the dim glow from behind it.

"I hope you all like it down here," a menacing voice called out, "because this is where I'm going to bury you."

Chapter 14

FRANK KNEW THE VOICE. It was Dave Gilson's—and Dave wasn't alone.

Gilson stepped into the tunnel, followed closely by two other guys. One of them was holding a short lead pipe. The other one gripped a nunchaku—a pair of foot-long pieces of wood, like sawed-off broom handles, linked by a short chain.

"We can take these guys," Joe whispered in Frank's ear.

Frank glanced at his brother. Joe could barely stand up by himself.

"I don't suppose we could all sit down together and talk about this over a cup of coffee," Kay Lewis said doubtfully.

Gilson bared his teeth in a vicious grin. "What's the matter, teacher? Is this class a little too advanced for you?"

While Gilson's eyes were on Kay, Frank slipped his foot behind Joe's leg and deliberately tripped him. "Sorry, Joe," he muttered under his breath.

He didn't think Joe would be much use in a fight right now—but he might make a good diversion.

Joe was still a little lightheaded, and Frank's move caught him completely off guard. His knees buckled. He stumbled back a pace, tottered, and collapsed.

"Joe!" Frank shouted, trying to sound surprised. "Are you all right?" He knelt down next to him, acting the part of the worried brother.

Gilson came at them like a shark catching the scent of blood and moving in for the kill. A switchblade flashed in his hand.

Frank waited a beat. He had to time this just right. Gilson was almost on top of him. Frank burst into action. From the kneeling position he spun around, pivoting on his left knee. He thrust out his right leg and swung it around in a swift, low sweep.

He caught Gilson just behind the ankle, knocking his leg out from under him. Gilson flew backward and landed hard on his back. His head smacked against the bricks. He didn't get up. He didn't move at all. He was out cold.

But the other two were closing in.

Kay Lewis jumped in front of the one holding the lead pipe. Instead of backing off when he swung the pipe over his head she darted in close, bringing both arms up and blocking the lethal downward blow with her forearms. Then her right hand shot out and up, and the heel of her palm smashed into his chin with shattering force.

His head snapped back, and he crumpled to the ground.

That left one. He rushed at Frank, whipping the nunchaku back and forth with blurring speed. Frank jumped up and back, dodging a forehand swipe. The chunk of wood whistled past his head.

Frank lunged forward, reaching out and grabbing the attacker's arm before he could lash out with a backhand swing. He tried to wrench his arm free. Frank held him long enough to bring his right foot up and smash it down on the guy's knee. He cried out and dropped the weapon.

Frank yanked the guys arm behind his back and slammed him against the wall. "If you even twitch," he said sharply, jerking the arm upward, "I'll snap it like a twig. Is everybody okay?" he called out.

"I think so," Callie answered.

"Everybody that matters, anyway," Joe added.

Someone let out a low groan. Frank looked back over his shoulder. Dave Gilson was conscious, but he couldn't move. Joe was sitting on him.

"Too bad I don't get paid overtime," Con Riley said as he slapped a pair of handcuffs on Dave Gilson and put him in the squad car. "With all the extra work you two make for me, I'd have enough cash to retire by now."

"Maybe we should just let them go next time,"

Joe replied. "Then you can get back to serious crime work, like writing parking tickets."

"Ah, traffic duty," the police officer sighed. "Those were the good old days." He turned to Frank. "What do you know about the other two perps?"

"Perps?" Kay Lewis said. "What's a perp?"

"It's short for 'perpetrator,' " Frank explained. "And the only thing I know about them is that they tried to kill us."

Con Riley pushed his cap back on his head. "Something doesn't add up. They're not part of the pack Gilson runs with."

"They're not Scorpions?" Joe asked.

"They used to be," Riley replied. "But Conrad Daye kicked them out. Those two are a couple of real lowlifes. Extortion, blackmail, you name it. If it's illegal, either they've already done it or it's on their 'to do' list."

"Why did Daye kick them out?" Callie asked.

Riley shrugged. "I guess even a punk like him has *some* standards." He handed a clipboard to Kay. "Now if you'll just sign this report, I can go put those animals in a nice, warm cage."

He paused as he was getting in the patrol car and looked back at her. "Are you sure you don't know what they were doing in your basement?"

Kay held up her right hand. "I give you my word. I have no idea what they thought they'd find down there."

* * *

Neither did Frank and Joe. And they were still trying to fit it all together when they got home.

"Okay," Joe said. "We know that Gilson got the key to Kay's place from Patrick Smith."

Frank nodded. "Smith was the realtor for the sale of the building. He should have turned over any keys he had after Kay bought it. But he easily could have kept a set."

"And we know that he lured Kay away so that Gilson could get in and out without being seen," Joe added. "What else do we know?"

"Whatever Gilson and Smith are up to," Frank said, "Conrad Daye's not involved in it."

"Hold on," Joe responded. "How do we know that?"

"You heard what Con Riley said about those two creeps that were with Gilson. Daye wouldn't have anything to do with them."

"So maybe Gilson only brought them in after Daye got thrown in jail."

"And how did the police catch Daye in the first place? Gilson was the only one who could have told them where he was."

"So what's your point?"

Frank looked at his brother. "I think Patrick Smith was behind all those attacks on Kay and the self-defense center. He hired Dave Gilson to do his dirty work for him, and Gilson set up Conrad Daye to take the fall."

"It fits," Joe admitted reluctantly. "With the heat on Daye, Smith would be free to carry out his plans—whatever they are. But it doesn't get Daye off the hook for kidnapping Callie."

"No, it doesn't," Frank agreed. "And it doesn't tell us why Smith is going to all this trouble."

"Maybe he's just following orders from higher up," Joe suggested.

Frank shook his head. "I don't think so. I doubt if Sam White would risk everything he's got for a few parking spaces. No, Patrick Smith is after something on his own. We just have to figure out what it is."

"Jake Barton's buried loot?" Joe ventured.

Frank sighed. "The vault was empty, Joe."

"Smith didn't know that," Joe argued.

"Sure he did," Frank countered. "Was Gilson carrying a pick and shovel when you followed him to the vault?"

Joe frowned. "No."

"So how did they get there? Gilson or Smith must have been down there at least once before."

Joe thought for a moment. "You're right," he said. "And the threats started as soon as Kay moved in—so Smith must have known about the secret entrance to the sewer before then. He probably stumbled across it by accident back when the building was for sale. He would have been in and out a lot, showing the place to people."

Frank sat back and rested his chin in his hand. "I can't shake the feeling that we're missing something," he muttered. "What does Smith know that we don't?"

"Real estate," Joe responded.

Frank sat up. "What was it Smith said about his computer system?"

Joe shrugged. "Something about being able to access any information in city hall that's available to the public."

"Right. Smith should know his way around the city's computer files for property taxes, land surveys, building plans—anything related to real estate. He probably even knows how to sneak in and out of some protected files without being detected."

"Like what?" Joe asked.

Frank smiled. "Give me half an hour and I'll show you." The last piece was falling into place, and he thought he could finally see the whole picture clearly.

Joe paced back and forth while Frank tapped away on the keyboard. Every few minutes Joe would glance at the computer over his brother's shoulder. Words and diagrams scrolled up the screen. More than once the message "Incorrect Password—Access Denied" flashed on the screen.

"Come on, Frank," he finally said. "It's been almost forty minutes. Wouldn't it be easier just to tell me?"

"Hang on," Frank replied. "I've almost got it. There!" He pushed his chair back and gestured to the screen. "Check it out."

Joe looked at the display on the monitor. "It looks like some kind of blueprint—except it's green on this screen."

"It's a blueprint, all right," Frank confirmed. "It's a blueprint for an underground vault."

"For Jake Barton's vault?" Joe asked in disbelief.

Frank shook his head. "Nope. It's for a *bank* vault. Bayport Savings, to be precise."

Joe stared at the screen. "The bank just up the street from the self-defense center."

Chapter 15

THE HARDYS HAD TO WAIT until the next afternoon to check out their theory.

"I'm telling you, Frank," Joe said as he pulled the van into the bank parking lot, "we should get extra credit or something for this stuff. For every case we solve we should get a week off from school. What do you think?"

Frank shot a sidelong glance at his brother. "I think I didn't haul you out of that vault soon enough. There's a short circuit in your brain."

"Hey, there's an idea," Joe said. "Maybe I can get out on some kind of disability."

Chet Morton was waiting for them by the front door. "This better not take long," he said. "I only have a ten-minute break."

"Wait a minute," Joe said. "How long have you been here?"

"Almost a month now," Chet answered.

"I mean today."

"Oh. Since just before two. That's when I start on Mondays."

"Why do you get out of school early?" Joe demanded.

"I'm on work-study," Chet said nervously, taking a step back.

"That's it!" Joe exclaimed. He turned to his brother. "Why don't we get time off for work-study?"

"Because we don't have jobs," Frank pointed out.

"We have a job," Joe persisted. "We just don't get paid."

Frank rolled his eyes and looked over at Chet. "Would you excuse us for a moment?" He grabbed Joe's arm and yanked him down the sidewalk. "What class is it this time?"

"What do you mean?"

"You only moan this way about school when you've got a big test coming up and you haven't studied for it."

"That's not true," Joe said defensively.

"Yes, it is," Frank insisted.

Joe looked down at the ground. "Okay, maybe it is," he admitted. "But I haven't exactly had a lot of time to hit the books while we've been on this case."

"Then we better wrap things up fast," Frank said, "so you won't have any more excuses."

"Hey, guys," Chet called out, "could we hurry this up? The bank's open only until five, and I've got work to do."

"Sorry," Frank said. He walked back over to

Chet. "Thanks for helping out. Did you get the information we needed?"

Chet nodded. "I counted the stairs down to the vault. There's a total of twenty-five."

"And the money?"

"They transfer the money out of the vault three times a week—on Tuesday, Thursday, and Saturday. But there's never much cash anyway. Most bank transactions these days are just electronic impulses. The money only exists in a computer memory somewhere."

"Don't they keep more cash around on paydays?" Frank asked. "Like on Fridays and at the end of the month?"

"A little," Chet said. "But people don't usually cash their entire paychecks, so we don't have to stockpile big stacks of hundred-dollar bills or anything like that. The most we ever have in the vault is thirty or forty grand, tops."

"Forty grand," Joe said sourly. "It hardly seems worth it."

"It's not exactly chump change," Chet replied. His eyes widened. "What's all this about, anyway? You guys weren't planning on robbing the bank, were you?"

"No," Frank assured him. "But we think somebody might be."

"Shouldn't we call the police?" Chet responded anxiously.

"Not until we have some proof."

"How are you going to get it?"

"We're working on that right now," Frank said.

"Speaking of work," Chet said, "I'd better get back to it."

"So should we," Frank replied. He turned to Joe. "Do you have the compass?"

"Right here," Joe answered, holding a round, flat black case in the palm of his hand. He flipped up the lid and took a bearing. "The self-defense center is down the block—due south."

Frank looked around. "Now we need a line-of-sight shot without any buildings in the way. Let's try it from the sidewalk."

They walked out to the sidewalk. Joe peered down the street toward the self-defense center. "Well, here's your clear shot," he observed, "but there's nothing to shoot at."

"I know," Frank replied. "That's why you're going to go stand on the sidewalk by the edge of the self-defense center." He pulled a small square object out of his pocket. On the top there was a digital readout and a single button.

"You're going to zap me with that thing?" Joe asked warily.

Frank grinned. "Don't worry. You'll never know what hit you."

"That's very reassuring," Joe muttered. He trotted past the four buildings that stood between the bank and Kay Lewis's building.

When Joe stopped and waved his hand over his head Frank aimed the device at him and pressed the button. A number flashed on the readout. "Move back a few feet!" he shouted.

"I want to make sure I'm getting a reading off you!" His eyes darted from the readout to Joe and then back again. As Joe backed up the number on the readout ticked upward.

Frank jotted down the first number in a pocket-size notebook and jogged down the sidewalk to join his brother. "From the bank to here is two hundred and seventy-five feet," he said. "I told you the distance meter would come in handy someday."

"Yeah," Joe said. "We might attract a lot of attention if we were out here dragging a huge tape measure down the street."

Joe knocked on the front door of the self-defense center. There was no answer. He knocked again, pounding harder this time. Still no response. He tried the doorknob. It was locked.

Joe looked at his brother. "I think there's one thing we forgot."

Frank nodded, a chagrined look on his face. "We forgot to make sure Kay would be here this afternoon."

Joe pulled out his pocket knife. "Do you think she'd mind if we let ourselves in?"

Frank glanced up and down the street. "We'll ask her later."

Joe flicked out the small blade and went to work. He slipped it between the frame and the door, just below the knob. He wiggled the blade around until he felt the lock bolt slide back, and with his other hand he slowly turned the knob and pushed the door open.

Joe looked back over his shoulder and grinned at

his brother. "She really should get a dead bolt."

They went inside and headed for the basement.

"Twenty-one steps," Frank announced at the foot of the stairs. "Chet said there were twenty-five steps down to the bank vault. Each riser is about seven inches. So we're off only by a little over two feet."

"Don't forget the three steps down on the other side of the secret door," Joe reminded him. "That makes it a pretty close match."

They passed through the double steel doors into the small side chamber. Taking the flashlight off the shelf and opening the hidden door, they went down into the abandoned sewer.

Joe pulled out the compass. "The vault that Gilson seemed so interested in is that way," he said, shining the flashlight down the dark tunnel. He glanced down at the compass. "That's due north. Right on target. And I'll bet it's just about two hundred and seventy-five feet from here."

"Let's find out," Frank replied.

Joe walked down the tunnel and stood at the mouth of the corridor leading to the vault that had almost been his final resting place. Frank took another reading with the distance meter.

"If this thing is accurate," Frank said, "it's two hundred sixty-nine feet from Kay's basement to here."

"We're six feet short," Joe pointed out.

"Not really," Frank replied. "We measured from the front entrance of the bank, not the side of the building." He ducked through the low opening into the narrow passage. "Come on. Let's take a closer look at the vault."

The pick was still lying on the floor where Joe had dropped it. Frank's shoes crunched on the shards of glass from the broken kerosene lantern. He looked down at the ground. "Give me the flashlight," he said, holding out his hand.

Joe handed him the light. Frank crouched down. He pointed the beam at the ground and brushed away some of the dirt and glass. "Look at this," he said.

Joe leaned over his shoulder. "What is it?"

"There's a wood-plank floor underneath all this grime," Frank answered.

Joe's eyes lit up. "Maybe Barton's secret hoard is under the floorboards!"

Frank rolled his eyes skyward. "Why me?" he muttered. He got up and dusted off his hands. "We're not here on a buried-treasure hunt."

"Sure we are," Joe argued. "The bank vault is buried, isn't it? And it's full of money, right?"

"Money isn't everything," a sinister voice replied.

Frank and Joe whirled around. Patrick Smith was standing in the entrance to the vault. In one hand he held a flashlight. In the other he clutched an automatic pistol.

"Of course, where you're going," he said with a mirthless smile, "you won't be needing much cash."

Chapter 16

"I SHOULD HAVE KNOWN you'd show up," Frank said.

Smith chuckled. "Yes, you should have. You're a bright young man." He stepped into the chamber, keeping the gun trained on them. "You're also incredibly predictable. I didn't just 'show up,' as you put it. I followed you here. In fact, this is exactly where I expected you to go."

He switched the gun to his other hand as he shrugged off a backpack. "I think you'll find that I brought everything we'll need to make this little party a real blast."

"Don't tell me you're going to kill us for a lousy forty grand," Joe said.

Smith turned on him. "I should kill you just because you're a royal pain," he snapped. He paused, and the empty smile returned. "But that would be a waste of manpower. You put me in an awkward position when you took my team out of action."

"Maybe you should have thought of that before you sicced Gilson and your other dogs on us," Frank said.

Smith shrugged. "David was expendable. He may be family, but he's just a common thug. He would have ended up in prison sooner or later anyway. Besides, I had a fallback plan."

He stooped down, grabbed the pick with his free hand, and tossed it to Joe. "And you're it."

Joe caught it reflexively. He gripped it tightly with both hands. The muscles on his arms bulged. He swung the pick over his head and charged.

Joe was quick—but he couldn't outrun a bullet.

A shot rang out, the sound a deafening roar in the confined space. Joe froze in his tracks. He looked down at his chest. No blood. Well, that must be a good sign, he thought. The gunshot was still ringing in his ears. But other than that, it didn't seem to have had any adverse effects on his body.

Smith leveled the gun at Joe's head. "I've marked the spot where you can start digging," he said calmly.

Joe turned and looked at the wall. The bullet had smashed into the brick at eye level. He realized that it had missed him only by inches. He glanced at his brother. Frank nodded.

Joe stepped up to the wall and started digging chunks out of it with the pick. There was a chance that someone in the bank would hear the noise through the two thick vault walls and call the police, but Joe knew it was a slim one.

Frank studied the older man. His opinion hadn't changed much. He suspected that beneath the surface there was nothing but blind greed. And he didn't think Smith was going to let them walk away after he got what he wanted. But the longer they played along, the longer they'd stay alive. And there were still some things he wanted to know.

"So," Frank said casually, "I think I've got most of it figured out."

"Really?" Smith replied. "Let's hear it." He sat down on the floor and gestured for Frank to do the same.

"You found out about the secret entrance to the abandoned sewer some time ago, back when the building was for sale."

"Go on."

"You explored it and found this old vault. But there was nothing in it. By the time you realized what was on the other side, it was too late. The building had already been sold to Kay Lewis."

"Pretty close so far. Then what?"

"You sent her some threatening letters, hoping she'd get scared, move out, and put the place up for sale. As a real estate agent, you could then pretty much come and go as you pleased."

"A crude plan," Smith admitted. "Also a very low-risk one."

"But it didn't work," Frank said. "So you raised the stakes."

"It was so easy," Smith replied. "I hardly

had to do anything myself. You see, David *likes* to hurt people."

"But you needed a fall guy," Frank said. "You wanted the police to suspect the Scorpions—but you didn't want any evidence pointing to Gilson. So you engineered the frame job against Conrad Daye. You told Gilson when to lift Daye's knife and where to plant it.

"And you supplied the plastic explosive that turned up in the alley. All Gilson had to do was steal anything with Daye's fingerprints on it. Like a shoe box."

Smith laughed. "You should have seen him when I handed him the stuff. He was afraid it would blow up in his face if he looked at it the wrong way."

He unzipped the outer compartment of the pack and pulled out a small plastic box with two loose wires dangling out one end. "Without a detonator like this you could jump up and down on a whole mountain of plastic explosive and nothing would happen. That's the first thing I learned in demolitions training in the army."

Frank didn't have to ask what else was in the pack. He had a pretty good idea.

Smith glanced over at Joe. He had made a fair dent in the brick wall. "That's good enough," Smith told him. "Now come over here and sit down next to your brother."

"I don't feel like sitting," Joe said in a surly tone.

"I didn't ask you how you felt," Smith replied coldly. "I gave you an order."

Frank looked at his brother. "Do what he says."

Still holding the gun in one hand, Smith reached into the pack. He pulled out a flat, rectangular slab covered with a thin cloth. He laid it out on top of the pack.

"Something tells me that's not a big bar of Turkish taffy," Joe muttered.

Smith slowly unwrapped the slab. It was the same mottled gray color as the plastic explosive Frank had found in the alley.

Suddenly Smith flung the slab at them. "Here! Catch!" he shouted. Joe dived off to the side, but Frank just reached out and snatched the slab from the air.

The realtor chuckled. "Well, now we know who listens and who doesn't."

Frank hefted the slab. It sagged slightly off the sides of his hand.

"Real funny," Joe said bitterly as he brushed the dirt off his jacket.

Smith waved the gun toward the hole Joe had hacked in the wall. "Fill it up," he said to Frank.

Frank knew what he meant. He got up and walked over to the wall. He took the chunk of plastic explosive and pressed it into the space. It was stiff but pliable, like a wad of clay that had been left out a little too long.

"Make sure it's flush with the wall," Smith ordered.

Frank pressed and patted the plasticized material until none of it stuck out beyond the bricks.

"That will do nicely," Smith said. "Now get back over here and sit down."

Frank did as he was told.

Smith rose slowly, holding the detonator in one hand and the gun in the other. He kept one eye on the Hardys as he stepped up to the explosive embedded in the wall. "Now comes the tricky part," he said. "It takes two hands to wire the detonator, and I can't very well trust you to stay put while I do this, can I?"

Frank smiled. "Sure you can."

Smith shook his head slowly. "No, I don't think so—and I don't intend to find out the hard way. So why don't you both just turn around and lie facedown on the floor?"

Joe glared at him. "And if we don't?"

Smith sighed heavily. "Do we have to go through that again? I really don't want to shoot you." He pointed the pistol at Joe's head. "But I will if I have to. Make no mistake about it."

Frank nudged his brother. "Looks like we don't have much choice." He knew they had to make a move soon, but not yet. He didn't like the odds.

Frank slowly turned his back to Smith and stretched out on the floor. Joe hesitated a moment and then reluctantly followed.

"That's better," Smith said. "Now just relax. This will only take a minute."

Joe turned his face to his brother. "Are we just going to do everything he says?" he whispered harshly.

"You already tried rushing him," Frank reminded him. "You want to try again?"

"But we've got to do *something!*" Joe hissed.

"All set," Smith called out. "On your feet. Let's get out of here."

Frank and Joe glanced at each other. This was their only chance, and they both knew it. Without a word they leapt up in unison and bolted for the steel door.

"Not so fast!" the realtor barked.

Joe was already through the door. Frank was close behind. There was an ear-splitting *crack!* and a piece of the wall next to the door exploded. A razor-sharp brick flake sliced across Frank's cheek.

He skidded to a halt. "Shut the door!" he screamed at Joe.

Joe whirled around and wavered. Frank was on the wrong side of the door!

"Do it!" Frank yelled.

"Don't even blink!" Smith roared. He grabbed Frank's collar and shoved the barrel of the gun against the back of his head. "No need to rush," he said. "We've still got plenty of time. So why don't you bend down nice and slow and get my pack for me?"

"Whatever you say," Frank replied in a strained voice. "You're the boss."

He stooped down and picked up the bag. Smith pushed him roughly through the doorway, following close on his heels. He slammed the steel door shut and leaned against it.

"Now what?" Joe asked.

Smith glanced at his watch. "Now we wait."

Joe had no idea how much time passed while they waited in the side passage of the old sewer. All he was aware of was the pistol. He waited restlessly for Smith to let down his guard, but he never did. Every now and then the realtor looked at his watch. Other than that he kept his eyes—and the barrel of the gun—locked on the Hardys.

Finally he checked his watch for the last time. "It's show time," he said, flashing a grin.

There was a muffled *whump!* that shook the walls. Crumbling bricks, dirt, and rocks showered down on them. Joe braced himself, expecting the tunnel to collapse around them.

It didn't. But Joe was pretty sure it couldn't hold up against another blast like that.

"Open the door," Smith ordered.

Joe grasped the handle, pushed down, and pulled. Smoke and dust billowed out. They waited for most of it to settle, and then Smith motioned the Hardys inside.

There was light streaming through a large hole

in the wall. On the other side was the shining interior of a bank vault.

Joe could tell it wasn't the main vault. It was the safe deposit vault. "Looks like your calculations were a little off," he said with a smirk.

Smith chuckled. "I guess I'll just have to make do with what's in there. Let's try box five hundred thirteen. That's my lucky number."

Joe stared at him, a puzzled look on his face. "What?"

"Take the pick," Smith said slowly, "and break the lock off box five hundred thirteen. Don't make me tell you again."

Joe shrugged and grabbed the pick. He crawled through the opening in the wall into the bank vault. The walls were lined with steel compartments, some big, some small. Each one had two locks on one side and a number engraved in the middle. Joe found number five hundred thirteen and smashed both locks with two swift blows. Inside the compartment was a metal box.

"Bring it here!" Smith called from the other side of the wall.

Joe shoved the box through the hole, and Frank took it from there.

Smith already had the box open when Joe crawled back through the wall. The realtor tossed his head back and laughed. The box was full of diamonds, reflecting the beam of the flashlight in a thousand colors.

Joe was stunned. "How did you know what was in there?"

"I know my clients," Smith replied.

"Of course," Frank said. "Sam White. Chet said he was one of the bank's most important customers. But he never made any deposits."

"Mr. White is a tad eccentric," the realtor explained. "He doesn't trust assets he can't see and touch. Everything he doesn't have tied up in real estate is right here in this box."

He slipped the box into his backpack and pulled out three flat gray slabs just like the one that had punched the hole in the bank vault. He looked at Joe, an evil glint in his eyes. "You were right. I wouldn't kill you for a lousy forty grand. But this is a whole different ball game."

He slung the pack over his shoulder and backed over to the door, keeping the gun aimed at the Hardys. "When they sift through the rubble they'll find a couple of inept burglars who blew themselves up in a bungled bank robbery attempt. By the time they figure out what really happened I'll be long gone."

He paused in the doorway. "It'll take me a few minutes to set the charges. That's how much time you have left to live. Enjoy it while you can."

Chapter 17

THE DOOR CLANGED SHUT, and Patrick Smith was gone.

Frank rushed over and examined the steel surface.

"Don't bother," Joe said grimly. "I tried that last time. It's just like the others. It opens from only one side—the *other* side." He poked his head into the bank vault. "Maybe we'd be safer in here," he said.

"I don't plan to wait around and find out," Frank snapped.

"What other choice do we have?" Joe responded. "I told you—there's no way out."

"There has to be!" Frank insisted. "Jake Barton didn't like dead ends. He wouldn't build a vault that he couldn't get out of somehow."

"Even if you're right," Joe said, "we don't have any time to find it."

"We've got more time than you think," Frank replied. "Smith needs enough time to get clear of the area. He doesn't want to get caught in the old sewer. The blast could bring the whole thing down. I figure he'll set the timer for at least fifteen minutes."

"The police should be here by then," Joe countered. "We must have set off some kind of alarm in the bank vault."

"And how long do you think it will take them to open the bank vault?" Frank snapped. "It's probably on a time lock."

Joe gestured around him. "Okay, you win. Where do we look? There aren't any convenient hinged bookshelves here."

"So we try the floor and the walls," Frank countered.

Joe tapped the wall. "It's solid brick, Frank. There's nothing here but . . ." His words trailed off. He felt something move under his hand. It was a loose brick. "What's this?" he asked, trying to pull it free.

He felt the floor drop out from under him—and then he was staring at Frank's shoes. He was still standing, but only the top half of his head was above floor level. "I think I found the other way out," he said. "I also think Jake Barton must have been a very short man."

Joe crouched down and crawled into the dark tunnel. Frank jumped in after him and handed him the flashlight. Joe thumbed the switch. A feeble beam flickered on and rapidly faded away.

"Terrific," he groaned. "The batteries are dead."

"Forget it," Frank said sharply. "Just go!" All they could do was blindly follow the passage wherever it led and hope for the best.

Joe felt like a rat in a maze as he scurried along, scraping his knees and bumping his head. The thought of rats made him shudder. "Do you think there are any rodents down here?" he asked nervously.

"You mean like rats?" Frank responded.

"Never mind," Joe muttered. "I don't want to know."

He crawled around a bend and saw a thin shaft of light. And bolted to the wall directly beneath the dim light was a rusty metal ladder.

Joe didn't ask any questions. He hurried over to the ladder and started to climb. It went up a narrow shaft. The beam of light was streaming through a small hole in a circular cover that capped the shaft.

Joe tried to lift the cover, but it was too heavy. Frank crowded onto the rung next to him, and together they managed to push it off to the side. They peered up over the edge.

They were in some kind of workroom. Tools hung neatly on pegboards mounted to the wall. A thin film of sawdust sprawled across the cement floor. And a man wearing protective goggles and clutching a whirring circular saw stared at them in slack-jawed amazement.

"What are you guys doing in my basement?"

he sputtered as Frank and Joe crawled out onto the floor.

A low rumbling sound came out of the shaft, and the ground shuddered under their feet like a mild earthquake. Joe looked back down the shaft. The bottom three or four feet of the ladder were buried under a new layer of rocks and dirt.

Frank stood up and straightened his jacket, ignoring the grimy splotches that covered it. "We're with the sewer police," he announced in an official tone. "Do you have a phone we could use?"

The man nodded dumbly and pointed to a wall phone.

Frank quickly punched 911. "Bayport Emergency," a voice on the other end said.

"There's been a break-in at the Bayport Savings Bank on Madison," Frank said.

"What's your name and phone number?" the emergency operator asked.

"That's not important," Frank replied. "You probably already know what I'm talking about. The break-in should have tripped the silent alarm. If it didn't, the shock wave from the second blast probably set off half the alarms in this part of town.

"What you *don't* know," he continued, "is who did it. His name is Patrick Smith, and he should be considered armed and dangerous. Have you got that?"

"Ah . . . could you stay on the line while we—"

"No," Frank said tersely, "I can't." He hung up the phone and turned to his brother. "We may still be able to catch Smith."

Joe grinned. "Let's do it."

Outside they found they were on Madison between the bank and the self-defense center. Flashing blue lights swarmed around the bank. A small crowd of local residents had already gathered at the scene, craning their necks to see what was going on.

"How are we going to get the van?" Joe asked. "It's in the bank parking lot."

"What are you guys doing here?" a familiar voice called out.

It was Callie Shaw, and Kay Lewis was with her.

"Callie!" Frank exclaimed. "I forgot you had class tonight. You're just in time. Give me the keys to your car."

"What kind of greeting is that?" Callie asked. "And why should I give you the keys to my car?"

"Because the fate of the free world hangs in the balance," Joe said.

"Try again," Callie said.

"Is this going to take long?" Kay interjected. "I've got a class that's going to start in a few minutes. The other students are probably starting to show up already."

"And the longer we stand around talking,"

Frank said impatiently, "the more time Patrick Smith has to get away."

"Then it looks like there won't be any class tonight," Kay said. "If you've got the goods on Smith, I want to be there when you nail him."

Callie looked at Frank. "If you want to use my car, then we all go."

"All right, all right," Frank conceded. "Let's go."

"So where are we going?" Callie asked as they all piled into her car.

"Smith's office," Frank answered.

"And on the way," Kay said, "maybe you can tell us what's going on."

While Callie drove, Frank described the events on the afternoon. Joe added a few details here and there.

"So what makes you think we'll find Smith at his office instead of on the next flight to Tierra del Fuego?" Kay asked after she had heard the whole story.

"Three reasons," Frank replied. "Number one, Smith has an inflated opinion of himself. He thinks he's sewn up all the loose ends in a nice, tidy package. He thinks he has plenty of time to make his escape.

"Number two," he continued, "if he disappeared right away, that would look suspicious. And that's the last thing he wants. Since he normally works late, he'd probably go to the office to keep up normal appearances."

"And number three?" Callie asked.

"I think we forced his hand," Frank said. "He had to make his move sooner than he had planned. That probably left him with some unfinished business."

"Like what?"

"I can't say for sure, but I know you can't just hop on a plane with a bag of diamonds and leave the country. It's not that simple."

Frank finished his explanation just as they pulled up in front of the office building. "Looks like you're right," Kay said, pointing to the parking lot. "There's his car."

"I just remembered something," Joe said as they got out of the car.

"What's that?" Frank asked.

"You and I can't go sauntering up to those video surveillance cameras by the front door. We're dead."

"You're right," Frank agreed. "We are."

"You certainly look the part," Callie observed.

Frank looked down at himself. His clothes were covered in dirt and grime.

"I'm still alive," Kay said. "I'll get us in."

Frank, Joe, and Callie stood off to the side, out of the range of the video cameras, while Kay pressed the button for Smith's office. There was no answer. She tried again. If Smith was there, he wasn't advertising it.

"Just start hitting buttons," Frank told her, "and keep trying until someone answers one of them."

On the fifth try the intercom clicked on. "It's about time," a voice squawked in the box. "How long does it take to get pizza around here anyway? It better be hot, or you can kiss your tip goodbye."

"Oh, it's hot," Kay assured him. "Just open the front door, and I'll bring it right up."

The door buzzed loudly. Kay grabbed the handle and held the door open while the others darted inside.

They took the elevator to the third floor. The doors slid open just as Smith came out of his office. He turned toward them and hesitated, shocked by the sight of the Hardy brothers.

Frank and Joe bolted out of the elevator and charged down the hallway. Smith reached frantically for the gun in his pocket. Frank lunged and grabbed his arm as he pulled out the weapon. Pulling the arm toward him and twisting his body at the same time, Frank flipped the realtor onto his back—but he was still clutching the gun.

Joe circled around to the other side. "This is ridiculous," he muttered. He leaned over and smashed his right fist into the man's jaw. Smith's eyes rolled upward, and his body went limp. The gun fell out of his slack fingers and thudded on the carpet.

"That's my idea of self-defense," Joe said as he picked up the gun. "Punching the other guy's lights out."

* * *

A few days later Frank and Joe paid a visit to the Bayport jail.

"Looks like I owe you one again," Conrad Daye said. "Thanks to you, they lowered the charge from kidnapping to assault."

"All we did was find out the truth," Frank replied. "I told you we would."

"What kind of sentence do you think you'll get?" Joe asked.

Daye shrugged. "A year, maybe two. Then five years probation, probably. All things considered, I'm pretty lucky."

"So are Dave Gilson and his two pals," Joe replied.

"What do you mean?"

"Smith needed some dead bodies to leave behind in the vault for the police to find," Frank explained. "And what better decoys than a couple of street punks with long arrest records?"

"But what about the diamonds?" Daye asked. "Once they cleared away all the rubble and discovered the diamonds were still missing, they would have known that somebody got away with them."

Frank shook his head. "Sam White couldn't prove what was in the safe deposit box. The police probably would have dismissed his claims as some kind of insurance scam."

"Gilson and company will do serious time for firebombing the self-defense center, planting the bomb in Kay's car, and attacking Chet," Joe said. "But at least they'll be alive."

"Well, don't expect Dave Gilson to thank you," Daye said. "Or Patrick Smith. He'll be a very old man before the door swings open for him again."

Frank looked at him. "Gives you something to think about, doesn't it?"

Daye nodded soberly. "It sure does." He glanced around the small visiting room. "I don't want to spend the rest of my life in places like this. Maybe I can use my time inside to finish high school. Then I can start over when I get out."

Frank smiled. "You do that—and we're even."

"I think I'll sign up for that self-defense course," Joe told Frank as they walked out of the jail into the warm sunlight. "I might learn something."

Frank arched his eyebrows. "I thought your education quota was filled up by schoolwork. What happened to the guy who wanted to take a break?"

Joe chuckled softly. "After this case, getting tossed on my back a few times a week by a martial arts expert will seem like a *vacation!*"

Frank and Joe's next case:

Someone's embezzling major league money from the minor league Bayport Blues, and retired baseball great, manager Stuart Murphy is the prime suspect. He wants the Hardy boys to clear his name—and as a sign of good faith, he gives them a vintage baseball card valued at $100,000!

But the boys face a dangerous lineup of hoods and henchmen who want the card at all costs. The game is heating up fast, and every pitch is down and dirty. Frank and Joe are right in the line of fire, and they'll have to come out swinging . . . in *Foul Play*, Case #46 in The Hardy Boys Casefiles™.